Christmas Sparks

I0619383

Book One of the Stonewater Stories
by
Ginny Frost

Copyright

Acknowledgements

This book would not have been possible without the love and support of my family. Thank you for not letting me give up.

A huge thank you to my beta readers—Jen, Grace, Ben, and Kari.

Dedication

For my father-in-law
    We miss you and your sharpie

Chapter One

Shin-deep in the December snow, Ryan Kramer wiped an ash-covered hand across his forehead. *Goddamn holiday fires.* Black smoke still poured out of the white colonial, despite the best efforts of the Stonewater volunteer fire brigade. The fire danced with a will of its own, sending thick gray smoke skyward. If the blaze spread to the second floor, he and his fellow firefighters were in for a long night.

Someone tugged on his jacket.

He glanced down at a soot-smeared boy. The child pointed to the house. His bottom lip trembled as a tear rolled down his cheek.

"My mommy's inside." His voice sounded raspy from the heated air. The boy dropped his hand slowly as ash and snow fell on his shoulders. His chattering teeth spoke more of shock than cold.

"You sure, bud?" Ryan knelt to meet the child's gaze. The little guy looked only about five or six. He and the other firefighters had cleared the house. Two kids, one woman. If she went back in... Ryan's pulse quickened as he prepared to don the ventilator again.

The boy stared at his home, tears in his eyes. "Yeah, I'm sure." The words were barely out of his mouth before a shriek pierced the air.

"Mikey! There you are." A young teen rushed over and crushed the kid in her arms. "Jesus, shrimp. I thought you..." Her gaze met Ryan's, and she switched to Indifferent Mode. "Whatever. You're safe. Stay here." Her words sounded aloof, but she didn't let go of the child.

Ryan touched Mikey's arm to get the boy's attention back. "Your mother, where is she?" The girl glanced around. Mikey pointed to the house again.

"Mikey." The teen knelt in the snow. "Mom went back inside?" He nodded, and she paled. The sound of breaking glass filled the air as a window blew out. Both kids flinched, huddling closer, tears on their cheeks.

Time to act. "Upstairs or down, Mikey?"

"Up?" he asked, his voice muffled as he buried his head in his sister's shoulder. Ryan glanced at the girl, who shrugged.

"Stay here," he ordered, waving an EMT over to the children. Dashing toward the house, he called to Chief Burges. "Woman, second floor." He tugged the self-contained breathing apparatus, or SCBA mask, into position over his mouth and slapped his helmet back on. After a deep breath, he burst through the smoky doorway.

Inside, thick gray clouds billowed from the living room. Two volunteers worked to contain the blaze in the room. He caught their attention, pointed at himself then the stairs. The guys paused for a thumbs-up.

A woman upstairs? How had she snuck past everyone? It didn't matter. He needed to find her, get her out.

Now.

Rushing up the wooden steps, Ryan almost removed the SCBA to call out. Taking it off inside a burning building was a violation and a stupid move. Somehow, he'd find her. His pulse quickened as he climbed to the top of the stairwell, instinct pushing him faster. Rooms stood to the left and right of the stairs.

He'd fought many fires in Meadow Wood Estates. The master bedroom always sat on the right side of the house. His gut told him to head there. Smoke gathered around his head. The door to the master stood ajar, and he nudged it open.

The murky room appeared empty at first glance. Stepping through the doorway, he peered through the haze, looking for any movement. A cough caught his attention. He swung around. In the dim light, he spotted a woman scrabbling through files on an old oak desk.

"Hey," he called, the SCBA muffling his words. "The house is on fire!"

She jumped, spinning around, her arms full of papers. "What?" she asked, blinking. Soot marred her pale skin, and ash and water spattered her clothes. Dust peppered her dark hair.

"You gotta leave," he yelled through the SCBA.

Tilting her head coyly, she said, "One second, please," The sweet, calm authority of her words stymied Ryan and he stopped in his tracks. Her reaction was the absolute opposite of what he expected. Then she flashed him a smile.

The simple beauty of it rocked him on his heels. All thoughts disappeared from his mind. He could only stare at that smile, that face, thunderstruck.

He almost answered, "Oh, okay," to her melodious and endearing tone. The crackling of the fire downstairs snapped him back to reality. Quickly, he crossed to the desk where she hunkered, sorting paperwork.

"I'll be two shakes." She continued to move and stack documents, adding more to the pile in her arms.

"Yeah, no." He wrapped his arms around her waist, lifted, and spun her around. *They don't call it a fireman's carry for nothing.*

The woman shrieked. Hefting her on his shoulder, he hurried out the door and to the hallway. She kicked, screamed, and cursed, her sweet, quiet tone replaced by something demonic. Twice while on the stairs, she almost hurled them to the bottom with her squirming.

All the fuss only made him admire her more.

"Lady, read me the riot act later." He adjusted her position, purposely bouncing her slightly. Papers floated around them.

"No!" Her voice cut through the air like a siren. "I need those. Stop."

Ryan continued down the stairs.

"Stop now." She commanded, and once again he almost obeyed. She kicked out, inches short of crushing his nuts. The glancing blow against his coat woke him from his trance.

"No," he said, adding authority in his tone. "Paper's replaceable. You aren't."

She huffed but quieted to a disgruntled mutter. Who was this chick? Sweet one minute, then swearing like a sailor, next ordering him around like a sergeant.

A call of alarm sounded from the living room where the guys still battled the blaze. A command, mixed with panic in their voices, sounded like "Gas line!" Ryan didn't wait to find out the rest. Gripping the woman tighter, he hurried out the front door and onto the lawn.

The surrounding air sizzled. Then a huge boom filled their ears. A wall of pressure smashed into them. His feet left the ground, and the universe clicked into slow motion. Acting on instinct, he twisted, curling the woman into his chest. She squeaked as they tumbled headlong into the snow.

His back crashed against the piled snow on the lawn. Her weight smashed against his torso, forcing the breath from his lungs. He closed his eyes for a beat, screaming a mental *"Oww."* When she groaned in his arms, his training kicked in.

Rolling over quickly, but gently, he placed the woman on the snow. He knocked off his helmet and shoved the SCBA to the side, scanning her up and down for injuries.

Haloed by the gleaming snow, the thirty-something woman with pale skin stared up at him. Her pretty face shone pink with exertion. Her brown eyes sparkled with unspoken fury, or maybe fear, as she gasped for breath. Papers scattered around her like rose petals on a bed.

Something deep inside him opened up and his heart called out. He swallowed hard, trying to resist the call of insta-love.

Leaning over her, restraining the rush of lust, he asked, "Are you all right, miss?" Her gaze remained blank, her lips twitching. He should've been concerned about a head injury, but his testosterone-soaked brain said, "gorgeous." It didn't help they were pressed together in the snow. "Miss?"

Slowly, her liquid brown eyes fixed on his, the faraway stare fading. With seemingly great effort, she raised a hand to his cheek, her face tilting slightly.

The instinct to kiss her surged in his chest and other areas, but he held back. Her lips opened, and Ryan believed he'd found the woman of his dreams. Rescuing her from a fire, saving her life...

She placed her whole hand over his face and shoved him away—rather unexpected, considering the romantic tension in the air. *Thank God, she didn't dig her nails in.*

Ryan's mouth hung open, words failing.

She, on the other hand, had no problem speaking her mind. "What the hell do you think you're doing?" She heaved him off her and stood up.

"The fire, miss. I... I was rescuing you."

She snorted, her hands on her hips. "I was fine. You didn't need to do a dramatic rescue. This isn't some romance novel." She marched toward the house, but Ryan caught her arm.

His desire dissolved into anger. This woman took the cake for belligerent rescues. "Did you not hear the explosion?"

Grabbing his arm, she hauled him to his feet. Ryan blinked at her in surprise.

"Are my kids okay?" Ah, Mama Bear Syndrome. He pointed to two small figures dashing toward them.

"Yep." It was the only syllable he managed before she turned on him again.

"I know you. You're one of those Kramers, aren't you? Figures."

Ryan stepped back. Over the years, his father and his contracting company hadn't always done its best for their customers. Ryan had left Stonewater to escape his family's tainted shadow. But now, it dropped over him again. It didn't matter he'd pulled her from a fire.

"Mommy!" Mikey slammed into the woman, wrapping his arms tight around her thighs. She wavered for a second from the impact. Kneeling, she engulfed the boy in her arms, kissing his forehead, checking him for injuries, whispering words of reassurance. But the reunion didn't squelch her anger at Ryan.

"Your family is responsible for this mess." She waved at the house. "It's December. My house blew up with everything inside. Our Christmas things are gone. Where will we stay?" She threw her chin up, glaring, but tears glistened in her eyes.

Dammit. She was out on the street with two kids—at Christmas. "Your husband?" he asked tentatively.

She blew a raspberry. An actual raspberry. "Now, what am I going to do?"

"Geez, Ma," the daughter said. "Give the guy a break. He did carry you out, caveman-style. Kinda sexy." She flashed her phone. "I got it on vid. Man, my friends are gonna freak." She turned her back on the adults, clicking her phone at the house, the firemen, and snapping several selfies.

"Jill, please." Her mother ran her fingers through her daughter's hair. "Oh, God, the paperwork." She sank to her knees and gathered up some of the scattered sheets. "If it's not here, if I could lose..." A tiny sob halted her words.

Ryan's heartstrings twanged again. He glanced at the woman, her two kids, and the burning house highlighting the snowy ground. Regret filled his gut. Having saved her life, he needed to go save her house. Before heading into the smoke, he asked, "Why did you go back, miss? For papers?"

She glared up at him, those brown eyes molten. Her nose wrinkled, but before she could speak, her son piped up. "You got my picture? Thanks, Mommy."

Mikey scooped up a crayon family portrait, complete with a Christmas tree.

She pushed a strand of hair away from the kid's eyes. "Of course, I did, sweetie."

Ryan gulped. A woman who'd risk her life for her kid's drawing...There was something in that—strong and a bit insane. His heart fell. It didn't matter. She'd hired his dad to work on the house. She'd never give Ryan the time of day ever again.

"I'll send the EMTs over to look at you," he said cordially, donning his helmet.

"I'm fine. Thank you," she spat, wrapping her kids in her arms.

Squeezing the children tightly, probably to Jill's annoyance, Margaret let go of some of her fear. The kids were physically unharmed, and if she'd grabbed the right papers, everyone was safe. Loosening her grip, she checked Jill's face, then Mikey's, for pain, fear, or anything needing immediate attention. Both looked shaken and scared but not hurt.

One worry gone.

She refrained from looking at the house. It was the least of her problems now. All that mattered at this moment was a warm place for her children to spend the night. Tomorrow, when her hands stopped trembling, she'd deal with the fire, the paperwork, and probably her ex-husband.

Scooping up Mikey, she used the last of her fueling anger to storm past the Kramer man. *Who cared that he looked sexy in the uniform?* And carrying her outside over his shoulder? She shivered from the remains of the hormone surge. No matter. He was a Kramer and a male. She had no use for either.

"Come on, kids," she said without looking back. She needed to speak with the person in charge. "You guys are okay, right?" Her voice stuck in her throat.

"Yeah, Mommy. Me and Jill ran out like you told us. We're fine." He squeezed her neck as they trudged back toward the house. She kept him facing backward, not wanting him to see the ugly black hole where their living room used to be. Jill never looked up from her phone. Margaret's heart squeezed. Jill would be fine. *Thank God for resilient teenagers.*

"Good." Margaret tried to mask her relief. The whole thing was scary as fuck. No crying, not yet. She'd cry later after she tucked the kids into a warm bed somewhere.

"Are you okay, Mommy? Because the fireman carried you out. So cool, but you weren't supposed to go back inside. They said so at school." He tapped a rhythm on her back, something he hadn't done for years. A sign he wanted some comfort.

She squeezed him tight, giving him the reassurance he needed. "You're right, baby. But I needed to get some things. Important papers."

"Like my drawing?"

She sighed, hiking him a little higher on her hip. Carrying him one-handed while she clutched the pile of papers wasn't easy. Hopefully, the file lay somewhere in the stack. If not, she and the kids were screwed.

Chief Burges stood next to the fire truck, shouting orders to men who scrambled in and out of the house. Margaret beelined for him. If anyone knew the situation, Harold Burges would.

A few feet from the trucks, Mikey slid to the ground, eager to check out the fire engine. Margaret glanced back at Jill, glued to her cell. "Honey, could you?"

Her daughter peeled herself away from the phone. Their gazes met, and thank God, the fourteen-year-old attitude vanished in an instant. "Yeah, Mom. I got it."

Margaret ran her hand over Jill's hair, and for once the girl didn't flinch. A thousand things passed between them, and her mom instincts told her Jill was dealing. Her daughter wandered off behind Mikey, watching both him and the phone. Pride surged in Margaret's chest at how well her daughter handled the situation.

"Chief," she said, "give me the bad news."

He met her gaze for a millisecond before focusing on the working men. "What caused the explosion in the living room?" He narrowed his eyes, but the warmth remained.

"Uh," Margaret racked her brain. "Oh, God, the fireplace. Please tell me it's not that." She hung her head. Her new fireplace, last year's Christmas gift from her ex. The damned thing had been the final straw in their wobbly marriage. Now the fucking thing had blown up her house.

"From what I can tell, you'll be out of the house for a bit. Call your insurance right away. Call Emil down at the Greenview Inn. I'm sure he can put you up, at least for the night."

She blinked rapidly. "How long?" Her words sounded strained, and she hated showing anything but her sunshiny kindergarten-teacher face in public. The divorce with Earl had pushed her to her limits.

"I'll know better once the fire is out. I'll have an inspector in there as soon as possible. We want you back inside, but only if it's safe." He tipped his head, a stern but understanding smile on his lips.

"We have a fire inspector in our little town?" With three thousand people in Stonewater, she didn't believe they warranted such a position. *Maybe they would call in someone from Iverton proper.*

Harold nodded to one of the men hauling a hose back from the smoldering house. "We'll probably make the new guy do double duty. Ryan, over there, is the town's new building inspector. He can check the place for us."

Margaret glanced back, trying to see who Ryan was. She knew most of the volunteers for the Stonewater firehouse since her son fanboyed about everything firefighter. The name "Ryan" didn't ring a bell.

"I'm sorry. I don't know..." She flashed her kindergarten teacher smile and fluttered her eyelashes.

"Ryan Kramer." He pointed. "The guy who hauled your ass outside." Harold grinned, his cheeks tinged with pink. "Sorry, ma'am. 'Scuse my language."

A Kramer, the building inspector? God, no. Kramer and Sons Contracting was the sole game in town. Many of her friends told her the company was hit-or-miss with projects. One week they'd build an amazing porch and patio, and the next week, a hot-water heater they'd installed flooded a basement. According to her next-door neighbor, it was never bad enough to lose business over. They always fixed whatever they messed up, but still...

Someone from Syracuse or Iverton might have been worth the mileage expense for Margaret's little renovation. But, of course, her locally grown husband wanted to hire from town. Earl assured her the Kramers could handle the living room upgrade, including the new stand-alone fireplace. Not that they needed it—the fireplace in the family room, attached to a real chimney, worked perfectly fine. But Earl wanted it.

He'd hired the Kramers to set up the hearth, build a mantel, add wall sconces, and install a giant TV which spanned most of the open space. Earl took the stupid TV when she kicked him out. The expensive, over-the-top device was the capstone of his surprise renovation. A surprise for him as she never watched the idiot box. Two children and a full-time job ruled out any TV watching.

"Oh." Her inviting smile faltered. *How did one of the Kramers end up the city's building inspector? Wasn't it a conflict of interest?* The only construction team in town now had city hall in their pocket.

"Margaret, you okay?" A hand fell on her shoulder. She blinked up at the chief. "You don't look so good. The EMTs should recheck you. You stayed in the smoke for a bit." He signaled to the medics.

"Oh, no." She pulled his hand down. "I'm fine, but surprised, I guess." She glanced around. Her minivan stood safe and sound behind the fire trucks, but the keys were inside the house. "Can we bum a ride?"

A weight hit her arms, and her papers scattered to the ground. A red-faced Jill stood next to her, a beige purse in her hand. Apparently, she'd hit Margaret with it. "Uh, sorry, Ma. I was trying to hand it to you."

Turning to her daughter, Margaret swallowed back her anger, fear, and frustration. "Did you go back in the house for my purse?" She gritted the words out between her teeth, not wanting to blast the girl. When the fire broke out, she'd shoved Mikey at Jill, commanding them to get outside immediately. She missed seeing Jill grab the bag.

With her usual sass, Jill bit back. "You're one to talk. You went back in for Mikey's pictures." She waved her hand at the remaining papers on the ground. "I was smart enough to grab your purse on the way out. I didn't risk my life..." She choked, her eyes brimming with tears.

Margaret gathered the girl to her and hugged her. "I'm sorry, baby," she murmured. "You're right. I never should've done that. I'm sorry if I scared you." She bit off the sentence before adding, *"but I needed the paperwork for all our sakes."* Jill didn't have to know what was at stake.

Her strong-willed teen wilted into tears in her arms. Margaret held her tight when another weight hit her legs. She folded Mikey into the hug, worry and fear filling her heart. What would they do now? What about Christmas? Damned if she'd allow the kids to stay at Earl's sad apartment in Albany. No way was he taking her babies at Christmas.

After a good twenty seconds, Jill broke from the hug. "Whatever, Ma. I'll be in the car." Shoulders slumped, she spun away, Margaret's purse with the keys inside in her hand. Fourteen had to be the hardest thing in the world to endure.

"Here, Mommy." Mikey handed her a fist full of crumpled documents. Harold handed her another, a worry line creasing his brow.

"Thank you both." She swiped at her eyes. "Mikey, we're sleeping out tonight. How about the Greenview Inn?"

Mikey's soot-stained face broke into a wide grin. "Will Emil make us breakfast?"

Margaret grinned back. Mikey's smile was infectious. "Breakfast and maybe dinner, if we ask nicely."

With a wiggle of pure joy, Mikey slipped his hand in hers and they trudged off to the car—homeless, almost penniless, in the December snow.

Ryan held back, waiting for the homeowner to leave the premises. She wrangled the two kids into a minivan. They needed a warm bed and a cup of cocoa ASAP. As the taillights of her car disappeared down Cardinal Drive, he headed over to the Chief.

"They okay?" Ryan asked, worry eating at his gut. *If my family...* he buried the thought. They'd find the truth tonight or tomorrow. He'd investigate the fire, if Chief and the mayor agreed. If Kramer and Sons Contracting put this family out of their house at Christmas time, he'd sure as hell do whatever he could to fix the problem.

Harold nodded, tracking the volunteers as they put out the last of the hot spots. "Electric or gas?" Ryan asked.

"I thought electric until the boom. I'll know more in the morning." The two men shared a look, confirming Ryan would investigate.

"Kramer and Sons installed the fireplace, huh?" Harold dropped the words with no judgment. Ryan wondered how many fires Harold had put out over the years because of his family's negligence.

"Probably. She was *not* happy to learn my last name. I don't recognize her. Who is she?"

Harold nodded to the mailbox. "Margaret Porter. She used to be married to Earl Porter. They split up last year 'bout January." He added nothing more. He didn't need to. Ryan remembered Earl from high school. He charmed the girls left and right, but he was also the laziest asshole Ryan had ever met. How could that fireball of a woman marry such a putz?

"They going to the Greenview? Any rooms left this time of year?" Ryan considered swinging by the Inn after they'd cleared the house, just to make sure the family had somewhere to sleep tonight.

The Chief shrugged. "Emil'll make sure they have a bed. Count on it." He gazed at the house. "Don't look too bad. Some plywood and plastic sheeting and they'll be back in a few days. Christmas won't be canceled."

Ryan nodded. "I'll look at the integrity of the wall by the fireplace. But Harry, the Christmas tree was in there."

Chapter Two

Margaret rang the bell at the front desk of the Greenview Inn. The delicate mahogany desk matched perfectly with the decor of the ancient Victorian building. Outside the building was a three-story gingerbread dream of balconies, tiny roofs, and odd-angled walls. It also had a portico over the main door to shield guests from the weather, a clunky add-on to the elegant building.

Inside, the painstaking work of the owners to restore the building was evident. It was a riot of flowered wallpaper, overstuffed tiny-legged chairs, and gleaming hardwood floors. It was the pride of Stonewater.

Over the years, she'd visited the place, oohing and ahhing over the beautiful interior. She'd heard the rumors about the food. Now she finally had a chance to sample Emil Russo's cooking. Silver lining and all. She sighed as she waited.

Fatigue itched at her and she considered driving into Iverton for a motel. Being so far from Stonewater would wreak havoc with their morning schedule. Glancing around, she caught sight of Mikey darting into the parlor, where books and games lined the shelves.

"No, Mikey, get back here. You're covered in soot."

"Oh, please don't sit, then." A voice sounded behind her and Margaret wheeled around, heart racing, nerves shot. A man in his twenties with brown hair stood at the desk, smiling. Patrick O'Hare, the co-owner of the B&B.

"Hi, sorry. I'm Margaret Porter. I teach kindergarten here in town. These are my children." She gestured at Mikey and the sullen Jill.

Patrick's smile brightened. He was a nice, down-to-earth guy, if Margaret remembered correctly. "How can I help you, Ms. Porter?"

Tired and frustrated, Margaret let it all hang out. "My house caught fire, and we have nowhere to go."

"Oh, my God." Patrick's hand rose to his mouth. "You'll stay here. We'll set you up and into a hot shower right away. Let me see." He scrutinized the reservation list. "Yes, I do have a room available but only for three days. Holiday season and all. Hopefully, that'll put you back on your feet. If not, I might be able to shuffle some things to get you more time."

Relief washed over Margaret to the point her knees almost buckled. "Three days? I think we'll require... my insurance... the house... I don't know how it is," she ended, her hands gripping the desk.

Patrick patted her hand. "Don't you worry. We'll even round up some clothes."

Margaret blinked at him. Clothing. She hadn't considered school tomorrow, and work, and... Her chest tightened, and she leaned into the counter for support.

No clothes, no money, only the car, and their shoes. Thank God, they had their shoes on. The reality of the fire sank in as her panic rose.

Patrick considered. "I can buzz Emily, my sister, and see if her kids..."

Jill broke in. "Chill, Ma. The house didn't burn to a pile of ash. Upstairs is probably fine. Living room, remember? Not a supernova."

Margaret wrapped her arms around Jill and squeezed gently. No nonsense Jill. Attitude larger than an elephant but practical as hell. "What do you suggest?" she asked, unwrapping herself from her daughter, who, of course, huffed loudly.

"I think we check-in here. Grab some grub, and call the insurance people. Like now." She held her phone out, a charger cord dangling from the socket.

"Did you grab your phone when I told you to find your brother and leave?" Margaret leaned in, but Jill seemed unfazed.

"Duh, I was on my phone when you yelled. It took three seconds to unplug it, grab Mikey, and your purse. I know how to fire drill, Ma. I've been training for years."

Margaret and Patrick shared a knowing look. He handed over an old-fashioned key to Jill. "Head up to room 201. I'll look for a cot for your brother. Your mom and I will settle here."

Jill grabbed Mikey's hand, turning toward the stairs. "Then food?"

"Yes, then food." Margaret glanced at Patrick, who nodded with a smile. "Go on up. I'll be there in a second."

"The kitchen is closed, but I could rouse Emil and..."

Margaret waved away Patrick's offer. "It's fine. Thanks, though." She handed Patrick her credit card, calculating how much money remained after holiday shopping.

Ugh—the Christmas presents, most of which were probably ruined. Hopefully, the Santa items in her closet had stayed safe from the smoke, water, and fire. She needed to go back to the house and see the severity of the damage. Once the kids settled in, Jill could watch Mikey for a few minutes. Margaret could use the excuse of getting PJs and toothbrushes from the minimart down the street.

Drained from the adrenaline rush of dashing back into the burning house, Margaret dragged herself up the stairs to room 201. The children were already inside, making a racket, arguing over something. The sound was music to her ears.

"Hey, kids," she said, entering the room. Both turned to stare at her, probably in shock she wasn't lecturing about how siblings are friends for life. Instead, she plunked down on the canopied queen bed.

"What a day." Margaret considered slipping off her shoes and burying herself under the handmade quilt that covered the bed. She indulged in the fantasy for a few seconds then returned to business. "What's the plan?"

Mikey hiked himself up next to her. "A bed for me."

"Or me," Jill shot in. "I don't want to share with either of you.

"Bed, check. What else?" Margaret considered grabbing her notepad from her bag. She had a dozen things for a list, and nothing felt better than ticking items off.

"Food," Mikey yelled with a fist raised in the air.

"Keep it down, shrimp. Other people live here, ya know."
Jill rolled her eyes and pulled out her phone. "We need
take-out. I am not eating in public looking like this." She spun
and headed for the small bathroom. "Get me a salad, 'kay?"
And she shut the door.

Margaret looked at Mikey who giggled and said, "She's
gonna be mad when there's no clean clothes to change into."

"You said it, kiddo. We'll wait on Patrick for the cot while
Jill cleans up. Maybe there are some clothes in the car."

Mikey snorted. "Just my soccer stuff, old and stinky. Jill
won't fit into that!" He rolled around on the bed. His shirt
hiked up just a bit, showing his round little belly. With all the
tension inside her seeking relief, Margaret couldn't resist. She
let the tickle monster out and attacked the exposed skin. Mikey
roared with laughter.

After a much-needed respite, with her son in her arms, she
picked up the conversation again.

"Dirty soccer clothes? Ewww. That stuff is still in the car?"
she asked. "We'll take care of that later. Once Jill gets out from
the shower, Mommy will hit the minimart and see if I can get
into the house for some clothes."

Mikey settled into tiny laughing fits as he calmed from the
Attack of the Tickle Monster. "Can you get our stuff, Mommy?
I'm askared we'll never see it again." He pouted, his eyes watery.

"Don't you worry, my son." She kissed the top of his head.
"Stuff is stuff. The important thing is we're safe. We can replace
everything." She smiled down at him, ruffling his hair.

"'Cept my drawing. It was so special you went back for it."
He looked up at her expectantly, and Margaret's heart lurched.

"Yes, honey." She kissed his head. "Yes, the picture. I had to save it."

Ryan toed a pile of rubble next to the fireplace. Grimacing, he shifted his clipboard to his other hand. He'd stayed to examine the structure. He desperately wanted to help, especially after the homeowner dressed him down. *Out of her house with kids, at Christmas? Not on my watch.*

A flash of headlights through the broken windows caught his attention. Carefully, he made his way to the far wall, avoiding the crispy Christmas tree. That and the blackened shapes below it tugged at his heartstrings. He and the other volunteers had tacked up some plastic sheeting over the huge holes once they extinguished the fire. Not the usual procedure but the Chief seemed to have a soft spot for the homeowner.

Ryan had personally explored the rest of the house, unplugging electronics, securing the water. Again, not the usual procedure. But as she had no help with either the kids or the damage, it was the least he could do. Plus, even with her coldness, she was smoking hot, and not because he'd pulled her from a fire.

Glancing out the window, he saw someone parking in the driveway. He secured his pen to the clipboard and headed out the front door, ready to speak to insurance agents or rubberneckers. Not as square-chested or big-boned as his brothers, Ryan could still hold his own if he needed to chase off trespassers.

A car door slammed before he closed the door. After adjusting his hard hat, he crossed his arms over his chest, trying to look formidable. "Excuse me," he called, "you can't be here. Leave the premises immediately."

A scoff sounded. "It's my fucking house, buddy. What are you doing here?" Ah, the kindergarten teacher. She strolled into the light of the porch. He loved how easily obscenities poured out of her when she wasn't being sweet and demure. He wondered if Harold knew about her mouth. Ryan certainly wanted to learn more.

"Hi. Mrs. Porter? It's Ryan Kramer with the fire department." He smiled. From her narrowed gaze, she probably only saw his silhouette in her door frame.

"You're still here? Ugh." She huffed as she reached the steps. Her disheveled hair and soot-spattered clothes gave her the air of a dangerous woman. The smoldering brown eyes and wicked stare added to her allure. He swallowed hard and tried to maintain his professionalism.

"Can I go inside? I need clothes and such," she continued, lifting her chin. The dark circles under her eyes hinted at exhaustion.

"Mrs. Porter..."

"Ms."

Ryan pressed his lips closed then tried again. "Ms. Porter, we don't know if the house is structurally sound. I'll need to inspect it in the daylight. I can't allow you up on the second floor or in the basement until I'm sure ceilings and floors are stable."

Her fierce demeanor crumbled in a heartbeat. "Please, I need some clothes for my kids. It's cold. They have school tomorrow. It's been a shitty night." She pressed her fist to her mouth.

Ryan stepped down off the porch and pulled Margaret Porter into his arms. He hated when women cried, especially single moms who had their Christmas set on fire. He wanted to help her, even if his family wasn't responsible for the fire. No one deserved to be in such a spot.

No one.

After a moment of stiffness, she melted into him. He squeezed and rocked her gently. "Give yourself a break here. You've been through so much today." He cooed the words into her ear and she hummed in response. "Why'd you go back inside anyway, Daisy?"

After a second, she shifted away. "Did you call me Daisy?"

He looked down into her endless brown eyes. The urge to kiss her rose again. Why would any man divorce this woman? Sweet, sexy, no fear. "Yeah, Daisy, short for Margaret." He smiled.

She studied his face, her arms still tight around his waist. "Yeah, right. Like who?" Her laughter, sweet and warm, drifted over him. The scent of roses and apples snuck through the odors of the fire, soot, and ash.

Ryan's head spun. *Like who?* He racked his brain. "Daisy Duke, from that old TV show."

She shook her head. "Seriously? You're comparing me to a young woman in tiny shorts?"

He searched again. "Daisy from *The Great Gatsby*? And some people called Thatcher that, too." He grinned.

"No, they didn't." She laughed, though, squeezing him tighter. Neither seemed to care if it was true. The laughter dropped the tension from her body.

Daisy? Who was he kidding? Funny and kinda sweet, but a Kramer which spelled trouble. She blinked, realizing belatedly, she stood in his embrace. His soft amber eyes searched her face, his smile warm, his lips inviting. It'd been a long time since she'd been in the arms of a sympathetic male. Did they still exist?

He'd pulled her from the fire and stayed here late and alone, inspecting her house. When he assumed she was an intruder, he'd even defended her door. Now he hugged her and graced her with an adorable nickname.

She blinked, an old fire reigniting inside her—a feeling she hadn't experienced in ages. Wondering what to do from here, she waited. Did people kiss when they felt the stirring, or was there more to it? She and Earl had dated exclusively in college. But the universe was different now. Jill would tease her to no end if she caught Margaret in the arms of a hot fireman.

Kissing him was a bad idea. His being a Kramer niggled at her. She never saw him personally work on the house, but with three or four brothers, how could she keep track? Earl went to school with them. He'd assured her they were the best contractors in town. Of course, they were also the only contractors in town.

Margaret stumbled back from Ryan's arms. No. If she needed to sue his family later, she shouldn't be making kissy faces with him now. Her nether region protested, but she wrapped her borrowed jacket around her tighter. "Can I go into the laundry room?" she asked. "And grab some coats, too? Everything's on the first floor."

Ryan's whole demeanor changed. He stiffened, and not in a good way—his body straight, his chin high. "Let me find those for you, Ms. Porter. Please stay outside."

She stepped forward to protest or at least tell him what to grab, but he'd already disappeared inside the house. An empty feeling rushed through her, the madness of the hug over. The magic dissipated in the chilly air and she mourned the loss of the moment.

After a few minutes, he returned with a laundry basket covered with coats. "How'd I do?" he asked, handing over the entire thing. She almost dropped it from the weight.

"What did you put in here, rocks?" she asked, setting the basket on the steps.

"Yes," he said. "Rocks and coats. As you asked."

She raised her head to meet his gaze and got caught in the full brunt of his grin.

Damn, she could like this guy, if he wasn't a Kramer. Maybe she'd use him for sex and move on.

Yeah, right.

She shuffled the coats and inspected the clothes beneath. Neatly folded stacks of pants, socks, undies, and shirts sat in tightly packed piles. Not a single towel or bed sheet tucked in. Impressive, considering he hadn't been gone for long. He found clothes for everyone and both kids' coats. She hated to give him credit. A Kramer, after all.

"This will do. Thanks, uh, Ryan, right?"

"Yes, ma'am." His response seemed formal. None of the sweet understanding or caring attitude she'd met with when she arrived. Apparently, he was done, too. She sighed, bending to lift the basket.

And of course, at the same moment, he bent as well. Probably a chivalrous offer to carry the basket for her. Too bad he hadn't announced his intention. The clunk of their skulls smacking together sounded like a shot in the quiet evening. Margaret uttered a grunt and fell back heavily on her ass.

"Oww, motherf..." She cut herself off, too big of a bomb to drop outside and in front of a cute guy. Blinking to clear the stars in her vision, she glanced over to see how badly she'd hurt him. He sat on his butt across from her, the big basket between them undisturbed. His gaze met hers before he dropped onto his back.

"Oh, my God. Ryan!" She scrambled around the basket. "Are you...?"

A huge bray of belly-shaking laughter erupted from him. He hooted, his hand to his forehead, out of control.

When he didn't stop, she asked, "Are you okay, or do I call someone?" She hovered over him and he roared on.

"Ryan!" She placed a hand on each shoulder. Could a concussion cause hysteria? "Seriously, are you all right?" She leaned low in the dim light, scanning his pupils for signs of injury.

His laughter died off to low chuckles. "What a mess, huh, Daisy?" He winked.

A giggle escaped her lips. He sat up and pressed his mouth to hers.

His slow, smoldering kiss burned her from the tip of her toes to the top of her head, leaving a crazy wildfire in the middle. She kissed him back, her tongue flickering over his lip until he opened, and she devoured him.

Ryan Kramer was a sweet treat—gentle and passionate in his kisses. Not demanding, not pushy, not at all handsy where she'd have to break it off and shove him again.

He kissed her as zealously as she him. In the heat and fun of snogging someone new, she lost herself. He was a good kisser too, not a slavering, gross, saliva-filled thing. She drowned in his kiss and wanted to stay there forever.

Chapter Three

"Heard you had some excitement last night." Ryan glanced up to see Mayor Denise Anthony in the doorway of his office, a steaming mug of coffee in her hand.

"Morning, ma'am. Yes, small electrical fire on Cardinal, the Porters."

Ms. Anthony probably already knew. She heard everything that happened in town.

Ryan tapped his clipboard. "I plan to stop by and inspect the damage. Hopefully, the family can move back in soon. I hate to have them out of their house during the holiday season."

She nodded. "Nice family, now that the husband's gone." She chuckled. "Let me know if there's any way we can help." She held up her coffee cup in salute and disappeared down the hallway.

Ryan gathered his things and headed out the door. Ms. Porter—Daisy—would be at school by now. He paused, one hand reaching for the phone, the other on his briefcase. Daisy and the kiss. His lips still tingled. Hopefully, he'd see her again soon, and maybe there'd be another kiss, or something more. He'd like to revisit the sweet scent of apples and roses and her luscious mouth.

The house stood alone in the morning light. The plastic sheeting stapled over the side wall had detached on one side and flapped in the wind. Other than that, it looked abandoned without its family. Ryan grabbed his clipboard and toolbox. He'd get to the bottom of it and put Daisy back in her home before Christmas. Maybe she'd even allow him to help repair the wall.

He used the keys he'd snagged last night to open the front door and headed to the living room. Daylight didn't help the mess. He glanced down at the half-burned Christmas tree, more determined than ever to find out if his own family caused the fire.

It definitely felt electrical. The far wall with an unvented firebox bore the brunt of the damage. A hole gaped open to one side of the mantel and another one engulfed the opposite side, straight through to the outside. Hopefully, Daisy had some good homeowner's insurance. Of course, if he found the contractor was at fault, then she might unload the bills on his dad in a lawsuit. His father would be pissed at having a lawyer sicced on him, but if Kramer and Sons were to blame...

A knock sounded at the front door. Ryan checked his watch. *Now what?* He'd just arrived here. Maybe it was Daisy. He hurried to the door. He opened it, and his jaw dropped.

David Kramer, his father, stood on the porch, a weary smile on his face. The man was dressed in his usual uniform of work overalls, with stuffed pockets, and a slightly too-small down parka, the same one he'd had since Ryan's childhood.

"Dad, what are you doing here?" No greeting, no hello. Too flabbergasted to be polite. The man shouldn't be here, especially if he was at fault for the fire.

Dad put his hand to his chin and his head swiveled from side to side, trying to peer inside. Ryan stepped forward, pulling the door shut behind him.

His father shrugged, shoving his hands deep in his pockets. "Thought I might stop by... Fire, y'know." A man of few words and no explanations. The years hadn't changed David Kramer much. "Electrical?"

Ryan drew in a deep breath. He didn't want to say anything, as things were still up in the air. But either way, Dad couldn't go in. "No conclusions yet. I've been here two minutes." Ryan refrained from throwing his chin up in a defiant gesture. The atmosphere felt ripe for a fight. He wasn't in the mood for another sore spot in their relationship. Things were tight enough.

"Yeah, I know. I saw ya come. I waited." His upstate New York accent sounded heavier with the tension between them. He hooked his thumb back toward the road. "We got a job at number twelve. Ted is on the way."

As if on cue, Ted's truck pulled up in the driveway. He swaggered out of the vehicle and joined the two men on the front porch. Ryan's chest tightened at the sight of his big brother. His and Ted's relationship was an ugly shitstorm compared to the quiet resentment between him and Dad.

"What's up?" He nodded his chin at the house. "You working?" He made air quotes at Ryan. "You could work for me and Dad. But I'm sure your inspecting is much more fulfilling." He thumped Dad on the back, a little too hard. Dad took the hit, flashing a smirk that Ted didn't see.

"Look, Ted, Dad, you gotta leave the property while I do my inspection. If Ms. Porter gives you permission to visit the site later, then fine. But right now..."

Ted cut him off. "What's your problem? We're here to say hi, to help out, and you pull a bullshit 'respect my authority' act. Calm down, little bro."

Ryan's ears burned. Once again, Ted belittled and insulted him for no reason. "Ted, I'm not going to fight. I need to inspect the damage and turn in a report. If I see Daisy, I'll tell her you stopped by."

Dad's eyebrows shot up, but Ted jumped in first. "Who's Daisy?" He started up the step, probably an attempt to intimidate Ryan with his slightly superior height. Ryan didn't move. He learned a long time ago not to back down to Ted, and he had the scars to prove it.

"Ms. Porter. Get her permission to enter the property."

Ted opened his mouth, probably to razz him about the Daisy comment again. Ryan cut him off for once. "I'll talk to you both later *if* we need to discuss the situation further."

His brother stepped back, frowning. Like a typical bully, he backed down when anyone stood up to him. "Fine. Be that way. Come on, Dad." He spun on his heel and stalked back down the driveway.

Dad glanced at his oldest son walking away. "Well, then..." he said in his calm, quiet voice. He stuck his hand out for a shake. Ryan grasped it, grateful his dad wasn't an asshole like his brother. "Be seein' ya." And he left.

Ryan watched him go with a pang of regret. In a perfect universe, he'd be part of Kramer and Sons' Contracting. He let himself back into the house, shaking off the ugly. The world was a flawed place, but damned if he'd put his tail between his legs for Ted or the company.

Chapter Four

Grabbing a stray soda can, Margaret glanced over the parlor. Their room upstairs was lovely, but at home, they had a three-bedroom house to roam around. Here, when things became tight, she and the kids would wander downstairs and hang out.

Margaret tidied the area. Jill and Mikey left tons of detritus—books, wrappers, and whatnot. She hated turning the room into their playroom, hated more the children didn't understand it wasn't their space.

"Where's your brother?" Margaret placed her plan book in her school bag. Teaching in December felt like juggling chainsaws. A good teacher kept a balance between holiday fun and actual learning. The children were so hopped up on December cheer that some days, breaking out the finger paint was the best choice.

Not that it mattered, with all the issues she was struggling with. She needed to feed the kids dinner and ensure they completed their homework—despite the fire, new location, and Jill's growing crush on one of the Inn owners.

Jill glanced up from her phone. "What?"

"Your brother?"

Jill sneered. "I don't know where the snot factory is. Why am I supposed to watch him every second? I have things to do." She stood and whirled out of the room like a tornado. Margaret smiled as her daughter stormed out.

Ah, fourteen.

Sighing, she turned to Patrick at the desk. "Have you seen my son?" She put a certain amount of pathetic into her words. Playing on Patrick's heartstrings wasn't a habit she wanted to continue, but he did have the best view of the downstairs rooms.

"He headed upstairs about fifteen minutes ago. You were kinda absorbed." He wrinkled his nose slightly but not in a mean or snobbish way. Patrick was genuinely nice. The nose twitch meant, "Oops, you didn't notice your kid. No worries," rather than "Wow, bad mothering."

"Thanks, Patrick." She tried not to sigh again or ask which direction Jill had gone. With one key per room, hopefully, Jill or Mikey had it upstairs. Being locked out would be a serious annoyance.

Climbing the stairs, she mentally reviewed her to-do list: insurance, call her ex-husband, Earl, and stay away from the fireman. The usual things. She'd barely entered the second-floor hallway when Jill came rushing at her.

"Mom, Mom!" she called, her eyes wide, her hands flailing. Either a boy called her, or something was wrong.

Margaret lowered her chin. "Spill." It worked for either situation.

"It's Mikey."

Margaret's blood pressure spiked. Pulling in a deep breath through her nose, she squared her gaze with Jill's. "What is it?"

"He's locked in the bathroom."

Margaret's shoulders dropped about six inches. Locked in the bathroom, no biggie. The boy did it twice a week. Jill usually didn't get so worked up. Placing a hand on her daughter's arm, she said, "Not a problem." They headed upstairs.

In the room, silence dominated the space. Strange, but not unheard of. Mikey might be playing with tub toys, dumping shampoo down the drain, or flushing the toilet paper directly from the roll. He'd only done that once, thank goodness.

"Mikey? She set her bag down. "You in the potty?"

A scramble of footsteps sounded, and the shadow of his feet appeared in the space under the door. "Yeah, Mommy. The door won't open."

She tried the knob. It refused to budge. "It's different than at home, baby. Turn the key in the lock on your side and you can get out."

"I gots the key, Mommy but..."

"But what, honey?" She kept the panic out of her voice, flashing of a thousand things going wrong with the key, with her kid locked inside a strange bathroom with razors and poisons.

"It broked. See." Mikey pushed half of a key under the door.

Margaret knelt to view the keyhole. Yep, something blocked the opening. "Can you turn the part that's left in?" she asked, a tiny bit of panic seeping into her words.

"No, Mommy." Mikey's voice sounded steady as a rock. "I can't grab it. I tried."

Jill hovered over her shoulder. "We could poke it through with a pencil or something."

"But how would we turn it?" Margaret considered. "Grab my school bag."

Jill did as instructed. "This probably happens in your class, right?" Worry tinged her expression, and Margaret patted her daughter's arm.

"I have safety locks at school. But we aren't stuck yet." She grabbed a ruler, a pen, and her wallet from the bag.

"So, MacGyver, Mom." Jill folded herself down on the floor next to the door. "Teach me your lock-picking skills."

Margaret didn't bother to roll her eyes. Placing the pen inside the old-fashioned lock, she pushed. A tinkling clatter sounded behind the door.

"The key popped out, Mommy. Now what?"

"Push it under, hon."

The other half of the key appeared under the door.

Disappointment filled her heart. The piece of broken brass would never fit in her side of the lock.

Time for plan B.

She tried to lever the ruler next to the lock, trying to pop it out, but the ruler was too thick. She grabbed a gas card from her purse and attempted to wedge it into the lock. After a minute of trying, the card snapped in two. She took a breath.

Mikey was fine.

It was fine.

Hinges.

She studied the frame, but the hinges were on the inside. No lifting them out. Blowing out a breath, she pushed down her frustration.

"Okay, Jill, head down to the lobby and ask Patrick for a spare key. Or another idea." Margaret fished around in her bag for a letter opener or bobby pins to pick the lock with.

Jill returned in a heartbeat. "No other keys. He asked if he should call the fire department."

"Oh, God, no." Margaret spat the words out before she even considered. Jill gave her a sidelong look.

"A hot firefighter might be helpful," she teased.

"A responsible fire chief might call child services on me for endangering my kids twice in two days." She rubbed her forehead. "Okay, Mikey. We might have to break down the door. But don't worry, baby. I'll have you out soon."

From the landing, Patrick's voice sounded. "Oh, please don't break the door. We just refinished those, and Emil will have my head. Nothing like this has ever happened here before." He sounded worried.

Margaret glanced back at him. What did he think they would do besides break in? She shook her head.

"You don't have to smash the door, Mommy. I got this." Mikey's voice seemed muffled. His shoes disappeared from view under the door.

"Sit tight, kiddo. I don't want you hurting yourself." She placed a hand on the smooth wood, trying to soothe her jangled nerves.

"Mommy, I can go out the window."

Chapter Five

Margaret's heart rate soared into overdrive. Gulping a breath, she tried to speak twice before she got the words out. "No, baby, not the window. Wait there."

"It's okay, Mommy. I can climb from the window to the porch thingie."

What porch thingie?

A clank sounded inside the bathroom. "I'm a good climber." Mikey's voice already sounded muffled. Another bang boomed inside the room.

Panic threatened to consume Margaret, but she shoved the sensation down. In her best mom voice, she called, "Michael Anthony Porter, you stay right where you are." Silence. She closed her eyes, and a tear trickled down her cheek.

All the crisis training from work—fires, active shooters, belligerent parents—kicked in. "Jill, call 911. Tell them a child is on the roof of the Greenview Inn. Patrick, get the door open now. I'm going outside to catch him if he falls."

Her voice hitched on the last word, but she still rushed out, down the stairs, and out the emergency door on the first floor.

Her mind whirled as she wondered what the hell would possess her son to climb out a second-story window. He must be heading for the room's balcony, which was a few feet past the bathroom window. If this was Earl's influence, with all the James Bond movies they watched together, she'd kill him.

Traversing the last corner, she spotted her little boy on the roof, with his arms wide open. She drew in a fluttering breath, wondering if she should call to him or let him be. He looked tiny, standing unsteady, and up so high. His face full of wonder, he was beautiful. But he'd look much better in her arms on the ground.

She raised her hand slightly toward him when he saw her.

"Hi, Mommy." He waved. "Told ya I..." And his foot slipped in the snow. His arms flailed. His mouth dropped open into a huge O.

"Mikey," she screamed.

Her little boy leaned backward, falling on his butt. He skidded forward and stopped with a jerk. His face paled, completely bloodless.

Margaret's heart stopped. "Don't move," she called. "Stay right there."

He nodded.

A white SUV pulled into the parking lot, coming to a halt a few feet away. Chief Harold Burges and Ryan Kramer exited the vehicle.

"What do we have here?" Harold asked, scratching his head as he gazed up at Mikey.

Margaret charged them and, as Ryan was closer, he received the brunt of her wrath. "Why didn't you bring the ladder truck?" She glared at him, a thousand poison daggers flying from her eyes.

Ryan didn't even glance at her. "Because Patrick said, 'kid locked in the bathroom,' not 'kid on the roof.'"

Just then, Jill spilled out the front door. "Ma, Patrick already called. They should..." She eyed the two men and pursed her lips. "Where's the truck?"

Harold sighed and reached inside the SUV. Margaret heard him calling on the radio for the ladder truck "A-SAP."

Ryan stared up at the boy. He rubbed the back of his neck. "Okay, then. Mikey, can you go back to the bathroom window?"

Mikey didn't even look. He shook his head, his chest practically vibrating, his fingers dancing a rapid rhythm on the shingles.

Margaret bit her lip. *God, don't let him hyperventilate.* "Sweetie," she called up. "The firemen are here. You'll be fine. Take a long breath and sit still. Okay?"

Pale-faced with two red apples forming on his cheeks, Mikey nodded. Leaning in, she whispered to Ryan. "Get him, now. He'll pee himself and then completely panic. That's his scared-shitless face."

Ryan nodded, not moving.

A fountain of fear rose from her gut, and she goggled at the firefighter. "Did I stutter? Go get him."

Ryan's gaze met hers, though his head still tilted up to the roof. "Ladder truck is over on Sugarbush. A guy putting up holiday lights got tangled, ended up hanging upside down from the chimney. They'll be here as soon as they can. In the meantime..." He glanced at the chief, who nodded.

"He can't climb back in the window." Margaret pointed to the second floor. "He skidded down the snow. He can't reach it now."

Ryan nodded again. "What room is that?" He indicated to the balcony. Margaret followed his finger. A red coffee mug sat on the railing.

Hers.

"Mine. 201."

"Be right back." Ryan ran into the building.

Margaret stood still, calling up reassuring words to her son, even though terror filled her whole body.

His little body began to tremble. Both fear and cold must be taxing him. Where was the ladder truck?

Chief Burges held his phone clamped to his ear. He glanced at her, a calm assuredness in his expression. Margaret wished she shared his confidence.

"Mommy," Mikey called. "It's not fun anymore. I wanna get down."

"Sit for a little more, kiddo. I think the ladder truck is coming. If you wait, you're gonna climb down the big ladder." That brought a slight smile to his lips.

Ryan appeared on the balcony. "Hey there, buddy." His voice held a warm smile. "Remember me?"

"You carried my mommy from the fire."

Ryan leaned over the railing, brushing the mug off its perch. The cup tumbled end over end in slow motion, until it exploded on the ground.

Margaret gasped, tears bursting from her eyes. Jill squealed and ran inside. Ryan looked at her, guilt all over his face.

Mikey didn't seem to have noticed at all. His gaze remained locked on hers. Thank God.

She smiled up at him. "Mikey, look at the firefighter." If only the truck would arrive, or at least Ryan had on his regalia. The uniform would calm everyone's fears, especially Mikey. But beggars couldn't be choosers.

Ryan called up. "I'm going to come over there, kiddo. Sit tight, okay?"

Mikey nodded, his gaze focused on Margaret.

Ryan slowly climbed over the side of the balcony. "Reach your hand out, bud."

Margaret's heart thudded in her chest. Was this the best way to get Mikey down? She glared at Harold, who put his hand on her shoulder, never saying a word.

Mikey blinked at him. Ryan reached out, flexing his fingers. Her son glanced down and Margaret nodded.

Gotta trust a firefighter, right?

Mikey lifted his hand, his little fingers inches from Ryan's.

With a breath, Ryan leaned closer to her child, one hand gripping the railing.

Margaret prayed the banisters at the Inn were as strong as the doors. Ryan reached over and snagged Mikey's fingers. She gasped involuntarily as he tugged, pulling her son closer. Mikey slid on his tush across the roof shingles. When Mikey was close enough, Ryan released the little hand. He wrapped his arm around the boy, inching him closer to the balcony.

"Now's the hard part, kiddo," he said. "We gotta climb back over. But I bet there's hot chocolate waiting for us."

Mikey nodded, his body pressed close to Ryan. Then he whispered something to his rescuer, who chuckled. Ryan heaved the boy over the railing, one-handed. His other hand still clasped tightly to the banister.

Margaret sighed in relief as her child disappeared into their room. Ryan grinned down at her, completely goofy.

Then he slipped.

His eyes grew huge as both feet went out from under him.

Margaret's heart stopped, her entire body frozen with terror. Visions of this heroic man smashing against the ground danced in her head. He couldn't fall, not after saving her family twice in one week.

She let out a squeak of terror as he jerked to a stop, emitting a hiss of pain. His hand was hooked around the railing, knuckles white, arm muscles straining. Quickly, he grabbed the banister with his other hand and Margaret remembered to breathe.

"What the hell are you doing?" Harold called up to him.

"Falling, sir."

"Well, stop. It makes us look bad."

With a groan, Ryan swung himself up onto the balcony.

Margaret stared at him, a whirlwind of emotion churning inside her. Her hero. Again. A rush of lust, relief, and something else poured through her veins.

She sprinted into the inn, taking the stairs two at a time. When she reached her room, Ryan stood in the doorway. She threw her arms around him and kissed him as hard as humanly possible.

At first, his body remained stiff, wooden. Then he met her kiss with the same wild passion she gave him. His arms wrapped around her, and he pulled her in tight.

She wanted every inch of him. This man, her hero. Rescuing her, her son. Almost crashing off a snowy roof. Her mind fogged under the demand of his kiss. She forgot everything but his mouth, lips, and tongue.

"All better," Mikey said behind them, and Margaret broke away with a start. Her child stood there, his eyes wide. "Did you kiss Mr. Ryan?"

"Uh..." She glanced from Mikey to Ryan to her son again. "I wanted to say thank you for helping."

"That was a *big* thank you," Mikey said.

Margaret gazed deep into Ryan's eyes. "Yes, yes it was," she said. "You okay, kiddo?" He looked fine, but with a six-year-old, you never knew.

"Yeah, I'm good. *Now.*" The boy grinned.

"Hey, bud," Ryan said, his arms still locked tight around her. "Find your sister and tell her you're okay."

"Sure." Mikey grinned. "You want to come, Mommy?"

"I think I need to say thanks some more."

"Okay then, but not too much kissing, because ewww." Mikey skipped out the door.

Margaret shook her head. The spell between her and Ryan had dissolved, but some of the magic lingered.

"Thank you for saving my son."

Ryan shrugged. "My job."

She sighed, resting her cheek against him. "It's all so..."

"Yeah," he said, his voice husky and deep.

She wanted to stay here forever, but real life stood outside the door. Time to deal with the aftermath. But this man, he pulled at her soul. She'd never felt anything like it before. The sound of Mikey and Jill celebrating reached her ears, and she let her shoulders drop. Reality called, and she needed to focus.

Remembering something, she changed the line of conversation. "What did Mikey ask you before you put him on the balcony?"

Ryan chuckled, a sly smile on his lips. "I'll tell you. But first, I want to know why you went back into the fire?"

She'd made peace with her stupid move. "Custody documents. Earl finally signed, but I hadn't filed it yet. With the crazy of the holidays, I put it off."

"Ah," he said, rocking her as they stood there wrapped together. "I guess they're worth going back for."

"It was stupid, and I..."

He pressed a finger to her lips. "You were thinking about your kids. But seriously, never do it again."

"No more fires," she said.

"Not that kinda fire, anyway," he said, running light fingertips down her arm. She giggled, unusual for her.

"What did Mikey...?"

"Oh, he required a change of pants, if you know what I mean."

Margaret buried her face in Ryan's chest, laughing long and hard. "I think we all do."

"Yeah, I hear you. But right now, I'm gonna have Harold check my shoulder."

"Oh, God." She backed up, keeping him at arm's length. "You're hurt, and I..."

"I want to make sure it's not too bad." He put his left arm around her waist. "Afterward, maybe the five us could grab some dinner."

"Five?"

"I can't ditch Harold. He's my dinner date." He grinned.

"Oh, really?" She raised an eyebrow.

"No, but he is my ride."

Margaret scoffed. "Inviting your friend on a first date after such a romantic, dramatic rescue?"

"Date?" he asked. "Huh." He seemed to consider it. "Even then, I don't want to be rude."

Polite, sexy, and a good friend. She could get used to a man like that. "I guess it's the little things, huh?"

"Always."

Chapter Six

Margaret rushed over to Stonewater Middle School as the buses pulled away. The insurance man said he'd arrive at the house by 3:30, and she didn't want to be late. She had called the school and told them not to put Jill on the bus. At her school, she'd barely retrieved Mikey before the buses left. You'd think the fire would be big news in a tiny town. Most of the staff didn't have a clue.

Anyway, it didn't matter. Her kindergartners behaved tolerably. Two spills at snack, and one potty accident. She loved the age group, but now that Mikey was older, bathroom issues were getting old fast.

Her son at her side, she rushed into the middle school office. "Hi," she said to the unfamiliar secretary—most likely a substitute. "I'm picking up Jill Porter." Glancing around, she marked the absence of her daughter in the room. "Where is she?" She tried to keep the tension out of her words. The adventure of the fire and the rooftop rescue had worn her thin.

She'd slept little last night, fighting with Jill for blankets, pillows, and space. At some point, Mikey joined them, and Margaret gave up. She hit the tiny cot the staff had dragged out for her son. Everyone at the Inn had been wonderfully accommodating, but getting another room in mid-December constituted an impossibility. The food was superb, though, and Margaret racked it up to breaking even.

"Hi, Ms. Porter," a young lady chirped as she swung into the office. The secretary made no eye contact with Margaret. "Whatcha doing here? Jill already left."

Margaret eyed the student. Annie? Amy? After a moment, she placed the peppy young lady as one of the few in Jill's inner circle. The girl probably knew her daughter's location. "Did she get on the bus, honey?" The kindergarten teacher persona slid neatly into place. "Oh, I hope not."

"Nah," the girl said. "Mr. Porter picked her up right before ninth period ended. I was running errands for teachers. You know, getting mail and delivering notes. I have study hall last period, and they always let me help because, you know..."

Margaret's patience ran dry. "You saw Mr. Porter pick her up? Her dad?" Damn Earl if he did. He wasn't supposed to pick them up at school without express written permission. Jesus, she didn't need this today. With the fire and the fireman and the insurance guy, Earl was the last thing she wanted to deal with.

She glanced over at the substitute secretary, who shrugged. Fighting over details with the woman seemed a moot point. Margaret grabbed the dismissal clipboard and yes, there in black and white, Earl Porter signed out Jill Porter. Groaning, she grabbed Mikey and headed back out to the car.

"Bye, Wendy!" Mikey called as they headed out the door.

"Who's Wendy?" she asked, fishing her keys out of her purse. Hopefully, Earl was at the house and the insurance guy hadn't arrived yet. She tugged Mikey to hurry him along.

"Jill's friend you were just talking to. You're so silly, Mommy."

She threw him a dark look as she unlocked the car. "Whatever, Mikes. We gotta get home." She tossed him in the back and jammed the keys in the ignition. Mikey scrambled into his booster seat.

"We can go home? Oh, but poop. I want to have more breakfast at the Inn. Mr. Emil makes the bestest food."

"One more breakfast." She pulled from the parking lot and leadfooted it to the house, praying there'd be nothing off when she arrived.

"Yay," Mikey yelled from the backseat.

Yay, indeed.

Several cars littered the driveway as Margaret pulled up. Her hopes sank. Earl's old van sat next to a newish sedan.

Great. Just great.

A third truck looked familiar, but she couldn't place it.

"Stay in the car, kiddo, while I check out what's going on." Margaret threw out the idle words, knowing her son would never listen.

He zoomed out before she even finished the sentence. He loved his dad fiercely and was far too young to understand the man's faults. And there were many, the fact that Earl had inserted himself here being her chief complaint at the moment.

Hefting her bag, she headed to the door, no sign of caution tape or anything else to block her entrance. She called after Mikey to be careful. Hopefully, someone in the house would catch her wayward son. She glanced in Earl's van as she passed. Jill's backpack sat in the front seat. A wave of relief rolled over her. At least she knew where her kids were. Earl might use this as a wedge for more visitation hours, or to blast her publicly, one of his favorite activities.

"Hello," she called, sticking her head in the door, feeling ridiculous for asking to enter her own home.

"Over here," Earl called back.

In the living room, a circle gathered around the plastic-covered hole in the wall. Earl and Jill stood in identical stances, hands on hips, heads back, except he had Mikey clinging to one leg. Beside them stood two men, dressed in shirts and ties, holding clipboards. One was Ryan Kramer.

Perfect.

She totally wanted her ex and new love interest in the same room.

No, not love.

Just lust.

She wasn't ready for love.

Not yet.

Mentally, she swore a blue streak. Taking a breath, she put on her teacher face and walked into the room. "What do we have here?" she asked in her cheeriest morning voice.

Half turning to her, Earl huffed, "We got a damn hole in my wall, woman. What's it look like?"

Margaret ground her teeth, ignoring his condescending tone. *Think of the children.* "A fire will do that, Earl," she said mildly.

He scowled at her, then focused on the two men. "Why they gotta bust through the wall to put out a chimney fire?"

Ryan glanced at her, and a sliver of heat danced over her skin. Funny how her husband never elicited such a response from her. But the fireman/building inspector did.

Great.

Just lust.

That was her story, and she was sticking to it.

He raised an eyebrow at Margaret, who waved at Earl dismissively. Ryan focused his attention on Earl. "Not a chimney fire. Electrical."

The second man nodded. Probably the insurance guy. "I agree, Mr. Kramer. We've seen everything needed to process the claim. I appreciate you being here for the examination." He put a hand out to shake Ryan's.

Margaret's mouth dropped open. Thanking Ryan, not Earl, felt very satisfying.

"Hold on there." Earl loomed over the two men, his arms crossed over his chest, his face set to "aggravated." Margaret shook her head as she assumed a spot next to Jill. Earl started winding up, and she prepped for a quick exit if she needed to get the kids out.

He glanced at the inspector with a tiny sneer. "The Kramers redid the whole wall, and you're telling me the electricity caused the fire. You sure on that? Because I'll sue his ass if his family did this to mine." Earl huffed, jutting his chin out. Margaret shook her head, hoping Ryan might see.

"Mr. Porter," the insurance guy began, "if there is any..."

"No, I wanna know now. Who did it to my kids, my wife?" He pointed an accusatory finger in Ryan's face.

"Ex-wife," Margaret said, with as much flatness as possible. She grasped Earl's finger and pulled his hand down. "It isn't your house anymore, Earl. You shouldn't even be in here without my say-so."

"But you let these yahoos in, didn't ya? Who knows what evidence he's planting to clear his father and brothers." Earl lunged at Ryan.

Margaret, recognizing his hot-air act, stepped between the men. Part of her wanted to allow him to push past her and let the cards fall where they may. But in front of the kids, no way.

"Earl, stand down," she said, placing her hands on his chest to "hold him back" as he expected her to. "Mr. Kramer is a firefighter. I'm sure he's here helping..."

"Actually, Mr. Porter," Ryan interrupted, "I'm the building inspector for the town, and I'll be in charge of determining what caused the fire. I will, of course, have a report for your insurance." He held a hand out to indicate the other man, who nodded politely.

"What a load of horseshit," Earl sputtered.

"Language," Margaret chided. She needed to put a cap on the nonsense, and quickly. "Jill, take your brother to the car, please, and get your backpack." She turned to the men. "Anyway, let's finish this up and my ex-husband can be on his way." She pursed her lips, tipping her head toward Earl.

Ryan caught her gaze and picked up the ball. He glanced at the insurance inspector. He'd met the man a half-dozen times before. If the guy's game remained the same, Ryan would be the one doing all the work and handing in the report. Actually, it made things easier, being in charge. But he hated handling difficult clients. He raised an eyebrow at Earl.

"I'll require some time to look over the damage before I send the paperwork." Ryan nodded at the insurance man, who chimed right in.

"And once I have the file from the inspector, I'll assess our cost, and what you'll be responsible for." The insurance man smiled weakly.

"My cost?" Earl bellowed. Daisy still held him back by one hand. Ryan admired the way she handled her ex. Many women he knew would have blown their stacks by now. It was clear she didn't want him here, but chose not to fight in front of the kids over penny candy.

"Sir..."

Earl roared at the insurance man. "Why the hell do I pay for fire insurance if you ain't gonna pay me?" He whipped around, pointing a finger at Ryan. "Your family's gonna pay."

Indignation rose in Ryan, but he choked back his anger. He glared at Earl. What kind of man screamed at people trying to help him? What kind of man behaved that way in front of his wife and children? In his head, he heard Daisy's deadpan "ex-wife" and he repressed a smile. *She must've had a damn good reason for marrying him.*

"Mr. Porter, if you'd allow us to do our work, we'd be happy to share our findings with you. If you're dissatisfied with the results, you're welcome to discuss the matter with the mayor. But right now, I need some space to do my job," Ryan said.

Earl relented, easing back from Daisy, and she dropped her arms. "I want the details, hear me?" Earl bellowed.

Ryan nodded, knowing he didn't have to say a word to him. According to Daisy, the house belonged to her.

Earl huffed again, obviously posturing. "You better." Not much of a threat, but Ryan set his chin and furrowed his brow as if serious, too.

"You probably want to take the kids for some dinner, Earl. Why don't you three head out, and I'll finish up here." Her voice turned sweet, very much the kindergarten teacher.

Did Earl know how much she manipulated him with that voice? Ryan repressed a smile.

"But I gotta ta—"

"No, Earl," Daisy said in the same sweet voice. "I've got this. It's all details. You go on, and I'll catch up with you and the kids at the Greenview Inn."

Earl's head snapped up. "You're staying there?" He started to bluster again.

She spun, placing a hand on his chest and he wound down immediately. Quite a sight to see.

"No choice. You herd them over there, and I'll be right along." She folded her hands but didn't move an inch. *Those kindergartners must jump when she talks that way.*

Ryan loved it.

Earl grumbled but called for both kids. He slammed the door of his van and sped out of the driveway. Ryan almost wished she'd forbidden Earl to take the kids. It didn't quite seem safe. But he was their father, after all.

Once the van left, Daisy turned to the insurance man. "I'm sorry. Earl doesn't own the house anymore. He forgets."

The insurance guy smiled and held out a hand. "Uh, okay. Then I'll be in touch with you, Mrs. Porter, about the claim."

She nodded, shaking his hand, and Ryan almost heard her think, "Ms. Porter." With handshakes all around, Margaret turned to leave as well.

"Daisy," he called, once the insurance guy, safely in his car, backed down the driveway. She stopped, her back stiffening. "Can we talk privately?"

"Not the best idea." She kept her back to him, a shiver shaking her body. Ryan wasn't sure the cold caused it. "The kids are expecting me." She waved.

He sighed. If he could have ten minutes with her alone. Just ten. To talk about whatever it was between them. He had to know if she felt it, too. The first kiss, then at the Inn. He didn't want the fire and the ex-husband standing between them.

"Maybe some time when the kids aren't around, then." He kept his tone light, hiding his desire. Being professional could be such a pain in the ass.

She peeked over her shoulder, a wry smile on her lips. Nope, not one-sided. "Maybe when they aren't around." Fluffing her hair, she hopped back in her car and sped off.

Ryan shook his head. If he'd met her before the fire, then... damn. Grinning like a fool, he put himself in check and returned to the task at hand. He and the insurance guy had looked over most of it, but Ryan needed to review one last thing.

Thus far, the inspection had flowed along easily. The sconces were clearly the source of the fire. Bad electric happened. But, crossing his fingers, he hoped a faulty light caused the blaze, rather than a faulty electrician.

He removed the blackened fixture and cut away the damaged drywall. Taking a slow breath, he examined the stud nearest the damage. On the wood, in clear black Sharpie, he found his father's handwriting. The marks signaled David Kramer had completed the electrical and installed the light. Ryan looked at the blackened wires, some without casings.

Dammit. Kramer and Sons were at fault.

He stepped back, cursing silently. He wanted to confront his father and brothers. Talk to them. Inform them that their faulty work left a family in the cold at Christmas. The mantle of guilt draped across his shoulders.

Chapter Seven

Taking a huge breath, Ryan knocked on Daisy's door at the Greenview Inn. His nerves danced. His stomach flopped. He'd waited an hour, to give her family time for dinner. Telling her quickly and in person was the right thing to do. A cold formal report might send the wrong message.

After a moment, she threw the door open. "What now?" Her voice sounded strained, and her cheeks flushed red. Ryan hardly noticed as the rest of her was wrapped in a big, white terrycloth robe.

He swallowed hard as his breath drained in a slow leak. Her wet hair and annoyed manner implied she'd left the shower to answer his knock. Her robe said, "I'm naked under here."

He forgot how to speak. Margaret looked him up and down, her mouth in a thin line. Slowly, her lips curled up.

"Sorry, Ryan. I thought you were Earl, bringing the kids back. I was ready to blast him."

Ryan bit back his news about the wiring. The bathrobe took precedence.

"Uh, no," he said, searching for syllables that didn't make him sound stupid. "You're alone?" He raised an eyebrow, conscious of how lecherous it sounded.

Margaret's grin brightened a thousand watts. "Why, yes. Wanna come in?" She slid to the side of the doorway, allowing him passage. He didn't run, but he didn't walk.

She closed the door behind him. "To what do I owe a personal visit?" Now that he knew her better, coy looked silly on her, and he grinned.

"No kids, exotic locale, bathrobe. How could I resist?" He stepped closer, wrapping his arms around her terry-clothed middle.

A laugh escaped her. "How could you know? Her arms snaked around his neck, her hips shifting to line up with his.

"Does it matter?"

"No." Her words breathless, she pulled him down for a deep kiss. His clipboard clattered to the floor, forgotten.

Having Ryan, in her room, at the perfect moment was better than a night alone with no kids. She kissed him like her life depended on it, all tongue and teeth and the warmth of his mouth. She was drowning, and he was oxygen. They stood locked together, kissing with a passion she and Earl never had, even on their best days.

Ryan's hands roamed everywhere except the robe belt. Such a gentleman. He obviously didn't have kids. He never experienced fast and dirty sex before the baby woke up.

She dragged her hands down his back, over his ass. He moaned into her mouth, squeezing her tighter. She let her fingers dance around until she found the tie to the bathrobe and released it.

Ryan's hands swooped inside the garment the second it opened. He touched her skin in light delicate sweeps, driving her crazy.

She had no time for foreplay. The kids, the maid, Earl might return any minute. Her hands already strategically located, she found his fly and wrenched it open.

"Daisy," he said, pulling back from the kisses, breathless.

"No time like the present, Ry." She winked, running her fingers inside his jeans.

He groaned, almost shocked but not enough to make her stop. He shifted closer, only to have her spin away.

Stopping next to the bedpost, she flung up one arm up to display the massive canopy. "Check out the beautiful, antique bed." Dipping her other shoulder, she allowed the robe to slide off her arm.

"Damn," Ryan whispered. "You sure?"

Margaret peeked over her shoulder where the cloth hung down. "Do I look sure?" She grinned and hopped into the bed. Ryan followed in her wake, crushing her to the mattress as they both fell across it.

He kissed her, his lips finding her collarbone, her shoulder, slowly moving down her body. Between kisses, he panted a few words, "I don't usually..." kiss... "this soon..." kiss... "but you..." kiss... "and..." He found her breast and finally shut up.

She moaned, grinding against his leg. "I don't usually go so fast either, Ry. But you are sex on a stick. I want you. Whatever you want to give. I'm yours."

And she realized she meant it.

She wanted him. For one night, or however long it lasted. The whole disaster with his family, Earl being such a dick, her divorce so new.

She'd spent too much time being a mom—to her kids, at her job which she loved with her whole heart, and to Earl, a child himself. She wanted Ryan to make her feel like a woman, a real person beyond the apron strings and the PTA. His touch made her feel alive, real, and if it was only for tonight, fine. But she'd make it last.

"Ryan," she whispered, tracing her hands over his back and into his hair.

He lifted his gaze to hers and those amber eyes said volumes. He paused in his exploration of her breasts. "Tell me what you need. Anything. I'll do anything."

Her body shook as his words sunk in. Not a promise she'd ever heard. "Even windows?"

"Even windows." His mouth met hers again, and his hands slid down the length of her body. "I hope this is what you mean by windows." His fingers settled into her cleft, slow circles that drove her mad. She groaned and bucked against his hand.

"Oh, my mistake," he said, sliding his fingers back. She gripped his shoulders, afraid he wasn't kidding.

"Ry," she panted. "Don't stop, don't..." But she never finished the thought. Her breath rushed from her in a gush as his lips brushed her thighs.

Ryan suppressed a grin as he kissed up her legs, using the tips of his fingers to slowly push her legs apart. The sounds emanating from her validated every feeling he had for her. Here was a woman neglected. Not just her house, and her kids, but her body, her soul. He'd wanted to be part of the solution. He wanted her high and satisfied, even if only for tonight.

She reacted to every touch, every caress with a boisterous energy he'd come to expect from the sex kitten hidden behind the kindergarten teacher façade. It didn't take her long to crash over the top—a long, low moan that shook the bed. He grinned.

"Oh, Ryan." Her voice throaty, sexy. With the job half done, he needed to make her come again, with him inside.

"Windows now?" He crawled up her body, enjoying every inch of it.

"Oh, God. Yes." She grabbed his arms and heaved him forward, his body covering hers. "Windows now."

He paused, a realization hitting him like a bucket of ice water. "I don't have any..." He waved a hand. "You know."

"Damn, I thought that's why you came here."

Ryan pressed his lips shut. Not the time to drop the bombshell. She might hate him later for waiting. But opening such a can of worms now? No way.

He started to sit back on his heels. "Well, then... I guess." He hated the disappointment in his voice.

"In my purse," she said, pointing to the bedside table. "Long story. Teenage daughter, sex ed. Big adult discussions. Anyway, in the purse."

He leaned over the bed, his fingers snagging a soft leather strap. Other ideas surged in his mind as he grabbed the extra-long handle. Shaking his head, he dismissed the thoughts. No time to explore the wild side tonight. He pulled the bag up and handed it to her.

She pursed her lips. "Seriously, you could've looked inside."

Ryan held his hands up, palm out. His father always acted like a gentleman to the ladies and taught Ryan to respect women. His brothers seemed to have missed the lesson.

Quickly, she dug through the bag, extracting an open three-pack of condoms. As she dumped the contents on the bed, he noticed only two fell out. He raised his eyebrow. Slapping at his arms, she chided, "I told you. Sex ed. And I threw the banana out."

He couldn't hold back any longer. The whole weird, over-heated, silly situation rolled over him. He fell back, laughter pouring from his lips. "Wow, not what I expected. Is the banana your fruit of choice?" He snickered into his hand.

"Wha..." She looked at him quizzically before it dawned on her. She poked his arm. "Mister, I'm not that desperate. I showed Jill how to put one on. I didn't use it for myself."

He barked with laughter, rolling onto his back. "And I'm supposed to believe you?" He knew it to be true, but teasing her was too much fun.

"Yes." She slid a leg over him, sitting firmly on his thighs.

That got his attention, the distraction from the condom search forgotten. Physically and mentally, he snapped back to the beautiful woman before him. His cock stood at full attention, inches from her thighs.

"Wanna see a demonstration of my skills?" His body strained as the words escaped her lips. She smiled an evil, villainous, wonderful grin. He'd remember that smile for years to come.

Flipping her hair back, she put the edge of the condom wrapper in her mouth and ripped it open with a twist of her wrist.

He gulped.

In a deeply erotic move, she slowly rolled the latex over the length of him. Her fingers brushed his skin from time to time, sending waves of heat up his body. When she reached the bottom of his shaft, she squeezed.

"Like it?"

He had no words, merely grabbed her arms and pulled her down on top of him. With a few adjustments, he thrust into her, finding the meaning of the word perfect. They moved together as if they'd made love a thousand times. She seemed to read him perfectly, giving and taking as needed. Totally in sync, they rolled over, and he pounded her into the ornate old bed.

Finally, Margaret threw her head back, her body squeezing him tight. "Oh, Ryan. Yes." And her words, her motions threw him over the edge he'd been teetering on from the start. He came, only regretting it ending so soon.

Panting, he dipped his head to kiss her collarbone. She squirmed and sighed. He wanted to stay there with her in that bed forever. The ugly news could wait another day. It was Christmas.

Margaret basked in the afterglow. Ryan had been so generous. Having two orgasms was simply unheard of. More than ever, she wanted Ryan in her life. Even if he was a Kramer.

After a few quiet minutes together, he stood and took care of the condom. She joined him, sitting on the edge of the bed, lamenting the loss of his arms. They'd figure it out, together.

"I, ah..." Ryan scrubbed his hair. "That was unexpected," he said finally.

"Tell me about it." She snickered. Sex in a B&B, with her ex-husband coming back any minute. She sat up straighter. "Oh shit." She jumped up, searching for her robe.

"What's wrong? Did I...?" The question trailed off as his brow furrowed.

"Jill and Mikey will be back soon." She gave him a look, hoping he'd understand her family couldn't find her with some man in her room. Especially if Earl brought the kids up. "Hurry."

Ryan seemed to catch her drift and searched for his missing pants. "Uh, I didn't think about... I'm sorry."

She tossed a shoe at him. "Don't be sorry. Be dressed." She rushed into the bathroom to clean up, hoping Ryan would pick up the slack. Exiting the room in record time, she found him hunched over the bed, dressed, adjusting the covers. More points in his favor. She blinked at him for a second, an image of him with her children by their Christmas tree. A buzz burned in her chest, and she forgot how to speak.

She considered throwing some clothes on as a knock sounded at the door. "Open up, Mom." Margaret turned to Ryan, the breath caught in her throat. She waved her hands frantically, trying to tell him to be causal, businesslike, aloof, responsible. He merely blinked at her and grabbed his clipboard. Where did that come from?

Dismissing the detail, she cinched her robe and called out. "Just a minute." She almost added, "Keep your panties on," when she realized she wasn't wearing any. Fluttering her hands at Ryan again, she pulled in a deep breath. It was no one else's business but her own. Hell, Jill would probably give her a fist bump over the conquest of the fireman.

Poised and ready, she opened the door.

Ryan hung back, standing next to the door, almost in eyesight, trying not to hide. He screwed his face up into his best "I have bad news for you, ma'am" expression and waited for the onslaught.

The boy rushed inside, hitting Daisy's thighs at a hundred miles per hour. She grunted with the blow, but took it like a lineman. Ryan suppressed a smile. The daughter strolled in, gaze glued to her phone. She easily detoured around her mother and brother, throwing herself down on the bed. Then the ex walked in.

Ryan swallowed and tried to bury his guilt. He didn't feel a bit bad about Earl. The ass let Daisy go. The kids were another story. Ryan shook his head as Earl marched up to her. The man was already talking as he entered, as if they'd been conversing in the hall.

"You see what I'm getting at, right, Margaret? Christmas, my place. I told you…" His words dried to dust as he locked gazes with Ryan.

Earl's brow furrowed, and his lips curled away from his teeth. "What the fuck is he doing here?" Earl didn't wait for answers. He took a giant stride toward Ryan, his fist cocking back as he moved.

Having older brothers paid off. Ryan ducked the first swing easily and caught the second in his free hand. "Mr. Porter? Your wife and I were discussing my inspection of the fire damage." He said it that way on purpose to appear innocent. He also waved the clipboard, a handy prop when establishing authority.

Earl blinked, tugging his fist back out of Ryan's grip. "Oh, yeah," he mumbled. No apology for trying to clock Ryan. "I… you two in the room alone… She's in a robe, and…"

"Jesus, Earl. Think for once? To say such things right in front of the kids." She tsked, turning to Ryan, a slight glare in her gaze. "And it's ex-wife, mister."

"Yes, ma'am," Ryan said, with a dip of his head. Apparently, he nailed the deadpan because Daisy put a hand over her mouth, probably covering a grin. He glanced away from her, not able to look at her without serious emotion pouring from his expression.

"Well?" Earl tapped his foot as if Ryan had kept him waiting for hours.

He turned the clipboard to face the man but held on to it. The explanation of damages was for Daisy's insurance, not his.

"You can see here," Ryan said, "the damage was due to two factors—faulty wiring on the sconces, and the extra wiring added for the additional electronics. I assume a TV used to hang over the mantel."

Margaret snorted at the same time as Earl launched into a description of an oversized screen with every bell and whistle available. *No wonder Daisy kicked him out.*

Ryan held a hand up to stop the outpouring of description.

"Okay. I see why they ran the extra electrical. But the wires were not insulated correctly, and the second point... the fireplace. Ventless fireplaces cause a lot of moisture. Exposed wires, moisture, and then fire." He tapped the diagram of their living room as he explained. "In addition, the gas line extension caused a small explosion. The main line didn't go up, and the damage was minimal." His first, and hopefully, last gas explosion.

Earl looked at him blankly. "Wha? Say again?"

Daisy dashed over, giving the man a slight hip check. "Let me see," she said to Ryan. Her tight lips and flashing eyes, telling him not to say any more to Earl. "Oh." She scanned the paperwork. "Will the insurance cover the damage?"

Ryan's skin flashed cold.

Time to spill.

He swallowed. "I believe so, ma'am. Looks like your installer is at fault." Slowly, he turned the pages of the inspection to the photos. He tapped on the third pic, the one with his father's idiosyncratic Sharpie notes on the inside of the wall by the wiring.

His father always jotted on the walls, the pipes—sizes, line ends, information to jog his memory later if he needed to do a repair. Or sometimes notes written for the homeowner to reference if they dug into the wall.

Most people who hired Dad appreciated these hidden notes, telling them the destination of the wire or the size of the pipe. But it also dammed his father as the culprit in the fire.

He didn't mean to share so much, especially in front of Earl.

"So, your dad fucked it up, then?" Earl snorted. "Guess I'll be suing his ass for all he's worth. Thanks for telling me, Kramer."

With that, Earl turned and left, no goodbyes or hugs for his kids, only a snort of laughter and some mumbling.

Ryan gazed down at Daisy, who looked back up at him, her brown eyes melting with sympathy.

"I'm sorry, Ryan. But don't worry. It's my house. Earl has no say in anything." She patted his arm and the guilt bit deeper.

"No, Daisy. If Kramer and Sons are at fault, then they'll make up for it. I'll break the news to my dad. It's the right way to do business. I'm not covering anything up." His last words came out harsher than he meant.

But Daisy didn't know everything he'd been through in Albany, as an assistant building inspector for a corrupt man. His boss insisted Ryan cover for certain contractors or bury the insurance claim for another. Thank God, the mayor pulled Ryan out before the pressure forced him to do something illegal. The guys who skimmed and cheated received a fine and were fired. Two faced an upcoming trial. Retreating home became a better option than hanging around in the midst of a scandal.

He glanced down at the papers. "I'm going to talk to my dad before I file. As a courtesy, because he's family. But I'm filing the report as is, with Kramer and Sons' faulty work as the cause of the fire."

"Oh, Ryan." Daisy wrapped her arms around him, and he accepted her embrace. They must have held on a little too long, because Jill interjected with "God, get a room." And they broke apart.

Chapter Eight

Ryan took a deep breath as he shut off the truck. He'd parked right in front of Kramer and Sons. Even with the early hour, Dad would be there. Ryan was ready for a quick getaway but also displayed his presence without fear. He'd throw the bad news at Dad and then submit the paperwork to the insurance and town offices. He only had to get out of the truck.

Sighing, he slumped in his seat. *Can Dad afford to pay for such damages?* It might start a domino effect, with other clients launching insurance claims against him. Would Ryan receive requests to inspect his father's work all over town? It was an eventuality that might sever any good feelings left between him and his family. At this point, coming home sounded like a terrible idea.

The rap of knuckles on his window rocked him out of his thoughts. His dad stood next to the truck, an enigmatic smile on his face. "'Morning, son," he mouthed.

Ryan exited the vehicle and hovered near his father. Words failed him. But as always, David Kramer knew the score.

He clapped Ryan on the back gently, not like his asshole brother's usual overpowered smack. "Come on inside, son. Let's get it over with."

"Dad, I..." The thought remained unfinished. His chin dropped as his chest tightened.

"If you had good news, you wouldn't be sitting out here. I can take it, son. Come on in." He tilted his head toward the back entrance and then walked ahead in his slow, methodical manner.

For the first time, Ryan sensed the weight of years on his father's shoulders. The man should be skating into retirement, not cleaning up messes left by his children.

He trudged behind his father, entering the back of the building, in the direction of the offices. Dad held the door to the clutter-filled space. Everything was labeled in black Sharpie. Ryan sighed at the damning habit. It helped when completing a project or repairing some earlier work. But this time, it sealed a probable lawsuit. Hopefully, Daisy would be kind and not bankrupt the place.

Ryan threw himself in one of the two metal chairs. His father closed the door. "Let's hear it," he said plainly. *Same old Dad.*

"Do you want Ted and Brett in on it, too?" Ryan asked, waving at the closed door. Ted meant complications, heated words, and accusations. He was so angry lately, but the man probably planned to take over the business at some point.

Dad broke into his thoughts. "It's still Kramer and Sons. He's a son. While I'm still head honcho, I'll deal with the building inspector." Not a drop of contempt in his voice, only his same plain, direct speech. Upstate through and through.

"The Porter place." Ryan fiddled with the clipboard.

His father held his hand out for the documents, and Ryan turned them over without a thought. His dad was honest as the day was long. Perhaps not the best contractor in the universe but a good guy. Ted was an angry mess lately. Ryan could hide the information from his brother until he filed the official report.

"Dad, it's the unvented fireplace, in combo with the wiring." Ryan scanned his father's face for a reaction. The man flipped through the report until he landed on the pages with the photos.

"Wiring?" he asked, holding up the clipboard. Ryan nodded, his heart sinking to his toes. "Huh." His dad pulled out a pair of half-moon glasses to inspect the photo. "It's my handwriting." He scanned the pictures, over the glasses and then through them. "And there's the date." He tapped the pic as he handed the clipboard back to Ryan.

He glanced at the photo, the date from last winter scrawled next to the wire's purpose in small, tight letters and numbers. "Yep," Ryan agreed.

"Yeah," Dad said, folding his arms. "The same day that idiot, Earl Porter, fired us. I'd labeled the stuff right before he stormed in, pissed off about the cost, the work, and the rush. He and your brothers were snapping at each other all the time. I told him if he wanted it done right, I needed a couple more weeks. The guy lost it. Tossed me and your brothers both out the door with our tools. I came right back here and wrote up a cancellation of contract, then got it notarized. Mailed it certified to the asshole. I wasn't going to take the fall for his crap. Not then, and not now."

Again, he said everything without a hint of inflection. All matter-of-fact.

Ryan blinked. The weight on his shoulders lifted. If his dad's company wasn't responsible... "Do you still have a copy of the cancelled contract?"

"'Course, I do. I been doing this for how long? I know how to keep everything tidied up. Your brothers sure as hell don't. That's why I'm hanging on. I leave, and those two jokers will have the place razed by Sunday."

Dad inspected the five filing cabinets in the room. Seeming to pick one at random, he sorted through the files. "Used to have a girl to file until Brett scared her away, flirtin' too much. The boy ain't never gonna learn."

Ryan swallowed hard. The two other offices held more file cabinets. Finding the right papers quickly seemed an impossibility. Ryan slapped his forehead hard. "Dammit, I told Daisy about the report in front of Earl. He's probably spent the day getting rid of evidence and making sure you take the fall for it."

"I'd like to see him try," Dad said evenly as he pulled a folder from the cabinet. "There ya go. All legal and pressing. I got the copy of the notarized stuff and a thing from the post office with the certified mail stuff. That all ya need?"

Ryan gaped at the folder, skimming through the contents. Canceled contracts, receipt of certified mail, phone log of calls to Earl and the permit board. Filed and in order. His father's diligence impressed him. Using the information, he could lay blame on the right person. Earl's word against Dad's, but with his brothers and the documentation as a backup, Kramer and Sons should be in the clear.

"It's perfect, Dad.

Chapter Nine

Margaret fidgeted with her purse as she sat outside the Building Inspector's office in town hall. Nothing made you feel like a kindergartner sent to the principal's office like sitting in a chair in a hallway. She'd wiggled out of a staff meeting to be here and forced Jill to watch her brother.

Ryan left a message at the Inn, asking for a meeting. Kinda odd. No personal phone call or contact. He'd even referred to himself as Mr. Kramer.

Not good.

She hadn't slept with him to get a good report. Other people might perceive it that way. That afternoon was only opportunity knocking. She liked Ryan, his heroism, his bravery, his cute butt. Hopefully, no one at the Inn heard their lovemaking.

Had Ryan been a one-off and now it was all business? God, she hoped not, but as she considered the cold tone in his message, her heart sank.

Earl wandered down the hall and threw himself in the chair next to her. "Good thing I stayed in town to help," he said, arrogance pouring through his words. "The Kramer idiot called me in, too. Don't he know it ain't my house anymore?"

Margaret said nothing. She stared straight ahead, avoiding eye contact with her ex. If he guessed about the tryst, even after Ryan had been so smooth at the Inn... She didn't want to think about it.

"I'm sure I don't know." Her words sounded stiff, but Earl worked her last nerve on a good day. Dealing with him during the disaster literally drove her into the arms of another man. Unconsciously, she crossed her legs. Earl didn't need to know anything about anything. Why the hell was he even invited to this?

After another minute, Ryan came down the hall, his arms full of paperwork. He nodded to both of them in a quick, curious fashion, and Margaret's heart hit her shoes.

A one-off after all.

Her first affair since she booted Earl out, her first since the divorce finalized. And it had come to nothing. Her stomach dropped. Somehow, their wild passion didn't last a lifetime. Biting her lip, she followed Ryan.

Earl bumped into her as she tried to enter the room. He shot her an obnoxious look. She'd forgotten he knew nothing about common courtesy or manners. By the end of her marriage, she'd questioned his upbringing. He pushed in front of her, taking the one other chair.

Margaret smirked, knowing Ryan could see her expression plainly. Maybe he'd rethink inviting the man here. She walked into the tidy office with binders, scrolls of blueprints, and filing cabinets. Ryan stood by his desk. Several folders lay on the blotter. He glanced up and frowned. Standing, he pulled his chair out from behind his desk and offered it to Margaret.

Okay, one point for him.

He moved back behind the desk, looking awkward for a second. He glanced from Margaret to Earl, then back to her again. She cocked her head expectantly. Ryan's whole demeanor changed. The tough, sure firefighter appeared in his stance, in his expression.

"Ms. Porter, Mr. Porter. I wanted to inform you of my final report for your insurance company. The inspection of 22 Cardinal Drive shows the structure is sound. I recommend repairs to the damaged wall in the living room before you occupy the building again. Also, keep the electricity shut off to that portion of the house until repairs are completed."

Earl broke in. "When do we get our money?" He leaned forward, his elbow on his knee, his chin in his hand.

The corner of Ryan's mouth curled up. "You're here as a courtesy, Mr. Porter. And to be informed of the situation. Now..." He shuffled papers on the desk, pulling a large report from the pile. He handed it to Margaret without a glance at Earl.

She pursed her lips as she accepted the report. Something smelled fishy here.

"The cause of the fire comes down to faulty wiring..."

Ryan didn't even finish saying the last word before Earl bounced to his feet, yahooing like some yokel.

Margaret rolled her eyes, not caring if her ex saw.

"When's your daddy writin' me a check, then?" Earl grinned like an idiot, and Margaret again questioned her choice to procreate with the man.

"Ms. Porter, here you see that the wiring for the additional outlets and lights are incorrectly insulated. The new unvented fireplace created dampness in the room and walls, as they do.

The brand you purchased is among the worst for moisture build-up." He glanced over at Earl, who scowled. Ryan remained professional.

Margaret studied the complicated report. She'd have to take Ryan's word for now, until she looked at it herself. Maybe even have a lawyer peruse it.

Ryan flipped to the pictures. "Here is where the contractor left off." He pointed to the Sharpie date, December 12, written on the inside of the wall. "Mr. David Kramer informed me December 12th was his last day on the job. Mr. Porter fired him before he finished wiring the new outlets and sconces for the fireplace."

Earl erupted from his chair. "Bullshit. He walked out on me. He left it unfinished."

Margaret and Ryan ignored Earl's protests. Ryan casually turned pages of the report in her hands. She kept her gaze on Ryan as a sheen of sweat broke out on her skin. "Earl fired the Kramers?" she asked.

"Yes." Ryan flipped pages. "Here is the notarized termination of contract. The dated photos were taken when Kramer and Sons Contracting left the job. I have statements from all three Kramers involved—David, Ted, and Brett, regarding the date of the termination of the contract and the status of the installation on that date."

Ryan's formality in presenting the information caused Margaret's stomach to flip-flop. It didn't feel right. She didn't know the man well by any means. And Earl attended school with him. There'd been rumors around town for years about why Ryan didn't work at Kramer and Sons—too good for it. He'd run off to Albany, to the big city, and left his family behind. Did he want to make up for lost time? Reconnect with his family at her expense?

She stared up at Ryan, processing only half of what he said.

Earl apparently grew tired of being ignored. He stepped in between Ryan and Margaret. "It's your goddamn family. 'Course they're gonna say what you want them to say."

She almost choked at her thoughts coming from her ex's mouth.

"Mr. Porter." Ryan stood to his full height. "I was not employed by Kramer and Sons, nor living in Stonewater when you terminated the contract. Mr. David Kramer kept meticulous notes on the incident. You can examine them yourself for their authenticity." He took a step closer to Earl. "I think you'll find everything is genuine."

Pulling in a deep breath, Margaret snapped herself out of the fog Ryan's words created. "Mr. Kramer, are you saying Earl is at fault for the fire?"

Ryan looked at her. His eyes seemed full of an emotion she couldn't put her finger on—sadness, fear, relief? "I'm saying, Ms. Porter, Kramer and Sons is not responsible for the damage." He glanced at Earl, then back at her. "Who finished the work on the walls and electrical?"

Margaret slowly turned to her ex.

Earl came up with the bright idea to make over the living room. He'd promised her a posh space for her book club and such nonsense. In the end, the room morphed into a man cave. She'd ignored most of the process, happy to have Earl out of her hair. But firing the Kramers... Who had completed the project? Because Earl didn't have a handy bone in his body.

"Your dad dropped the ball on the project. What could I do? Let the walls sit there open? Let my boy touch those wires?" Earl crossed his arms. "Nah, your family's gonna pay for the fire. I'll tell you what." He headed toward the door.

Ryan shot out an arm to stop his exit. "Mr. Porter, understand all the information will be in the official report I give to the insurance company." Ryan raised his chin, authority pouring from him.

Earl scoffed as Margaret expected. "You go right ahead. I'll sue their ass and yours too, pencil pusher." He moved to shove Ryan but seemed to think better of it. Perhaps he remembered how easily Ryan had dodged his fists at the Inn. "Whatever," Earl finished, his usual last statement when he knew he'd lost the argument.

Ryan closed the door behind him. He spoke again, in quiet tones, but Margaret's brain refused to engage. Earl was at fault for the fire? He was the one who finished the remodel, wired the outlets, and installed the unvented fireplace. He sealed up the walls with the unfinished electrical work and left it. The wall next to the new lights definitely had looked lumpy.

She'd never questioned it. She'd allowed Earl to do as he pleased while she worked. The new room... Deep down, she knew it'd be a disaster. But it gave her time to decide what to do about their failing marriage.

He worked on it for three months. She didn't remember when the Kramers stopped coming. She glanced down at the report. The date stood out in bold black and white. December, weeks before he presented the remodel to her with the fucking TV. The leather recliners and mini fridge didn't help matters. But the giant TV she'd already told him was beyond her kindergarten teacher's budget hung on the wall. And with the Christmas bills rolling in... She'd tossed him out that morning, screaming and swearing for him to take the TV before she smashed it.

And he left.

His friends arrived the next day, taking apart the mancave and half the bedroom. In a flash, Earl was gone. She served him the divorce papers she'd already drawn up. Not wanting to spoil the holidays, but also not wanting to wait another second.

Now, in the office of the man she'd just slept with, another monkey wrench found its way into her gears. Earl caused the fire, and he had no money. Hell, child support payments hardly ever arrived. There was little hope he'd buy anything for the kids for Christmas. Her insurance would have to cover the water, smoke, and fire damage, then pay for new electrical and the removal of the damned fireplace. And now they might not pay. Not if Earl was liable. He lived there at the time. It was still his house last December.

Tears burned in her eyes as her brain finally tuned in on Ryan's words. He talked on as if his words hadn't been devastating. "I'll talk to the guy personally. I'm sure he'll be able to recommend some action where..."

In the pit of her stomach, a fire erupted. With the most calm she could muster, Margaret rose from her seat.

Here was the man who conveniently shared all that information with Earl, invited him to the meeting, showed him the report. Ryan had no right.

She pushed the report back at Ryan. "What you're telling me is that with two weeks 'til Christmas, my ex-husband is responsible for the fire that caused the gaping hole in my house.

And my insurance won't cover the cost of the damage. Is that what you're saying?" She raised her gaze to his, disappointment filling her heart.

He'd said all this to Earl, not met with her separately or first. He protected his family at the cost of hers.

It dawned on her that she'd made a terrible error in judgment once again. Fell into bed with the wrong man at the wrong time. At least this time, there wouldn't be a little Jill along in nine months.

Ryan's mouth dropped open, but no words came out. He blinked at her, as if amazed she understood his position.

"Oh, and your family gets off free and clear." She pressed her hand against his chest, not quite a shove. "You're still shiny and perfect with your cushy new job after you skittered home from Albany." She pushed harder. "And I'm left with a bigger mess than before because you couldn't keep it in your pants." She put her full weight into her palms, shoving him backward toward the desk.

But she'd been the one pushing for sex...

Loathing, regret, and chagrin raced through her. The parade of emotions said one thing: she was stupid.

After everything she'd been through with Earl, was any man worth a hill of beans? She'd never found one who'd stand by his word, work hard, and be a good person. How could she have ever thought Ryan was different?

"It's not like that. You have no idea the hell I went through in Albany, the corruption, the pressure to take bribes and kickbacks. That's why I have to report the truth. Yes, it vindicates my dad, but I'm not trying to vilify your ex. What's important is to repair the damage..." He reached out for her, but she stepped back from him.

"Damage? What do you know about damage? You've met my kids. You saw the fire. No Christmas. No money for presents, and who the hell am I going to hire to fix the wall? Your father?"

She threw her head back and laughed long and hard. The outburst helped streamline her emotions into one long fuse of anger. "You've no idea what you've done. You don't know the real damage you've caused. Thanks so fucking much, Mr. Kramer." She spun to leave as his hand landed on her shoulder.

"Daisy..."

She shoved him away, unable to face him. Her emotions switched gears again, her anger bubbling over into tears and shame. "Don't you call me that. Don't you dare." She launched out the door, ignoring his pleas to come back.

Chapter Ten

How had he not seen this outcome? Ryan sank into his desk chair, his head in his hands. Of course, Daisy would have to pay for it. His brain must have equated responsibility with a male, not the head of household. Which meant her, not Earl.

It sounded like the man didn't pay for anything, not even child support. She'd never be able to make him help with the damage to the house—not without a serious legal battle. Kramer and Sons didn't fail, but the actual proof that Earl finished the project himself didn't exist. He and his buddies might have done it. And if they remained the same guys from high school, they'd never rat each other out.

Now Margaret would be forced to pay for thousands of dollars in repairs for something her moron of an ex-husband had done.

Ryan shook his head. How could he have been so thick? He should've talked to her first, found a way to pin the blame on the right person, and make him pay. There was no win here. If his dad's company had been responsible, he'd be up the same creek. A lawsuit and the association with a fire during the holidays might bury Kramer and Sons permanently.

Sighing, he straightened. He wanted to do something, without it appearing to be favoritism or a payoff. Being the building inspector had to have some power in this little town. He'd had enough drama and corruption in Albany and didn't want to soil things in Stonewater.

Resigning might be the best option, but it solved nothing. The next inspector would find the same things. Either Earl or Dad was at fault. And all evidence pointed to Earl, every bit of it circumstantial.

A knock sounded at his door and Ted pushed inside. He stood tall, highlighting his high school football physique. "There you are."

Ryan raised an eyebrow. Where else would he be?

Ted continued, "You better settle the fire crap right now, little bro. I don't care if you're banging that chick or not. We ain't gonna take the fall."

Dad skirted in behind Ted, a smirk on his lips. He said nothing as he plopped into the chair. He stretched his legs out, crossed at the ankle. With a beer in his hand, he'd be ready to watch a game. Perhaps he was. Their gazes met for a brief second before Ted stormed over them again.

"Dad said he gave you the Porter file, and you took it. What the fuck? Ever heard of a copy machine?" Ted paced the room, his arms flapping. The words *drama queen* in Jill Porter's voice rang in his head. He stifled a grin. Dad caught the expression and smiled himself.

Ryan picked up Dad's file from his desk. "Here you are," he said, not falling into Ted's usual game.

Ted grabbed the paperwork, huffing, and flipped through it. "How do I know you didn't mess with this to clear your little girlfriend?" He poked Ryan with the folder.

Ryan rolled his chair back an inch or two, out of Ted's reach.

"It's all in there. Dad can verify." He put his elbows on the arms of the chair, tenting his fingers over his lap, the epitome of calm and collected.

Ted tossed the file at Dad who caught it deftly as his brother raged on, "We got canned from the job, but you better not go around telling everyone. We got a reputation to uphold. No thanks to you. You should be on this side of the desk with us."

Dad held up a hand and Ted wound down some. "It's all here, Ted. The information about the cancellation of the contract, notarized and legal." He snapped the folder shut. "I assume you got a copy, son?" He pointed the folder at Ryan, who nodded. "Then we're done here." He stood and faced Ted.

"Ryan ain't answered a damn thing, Dad. We're not leaving until he tells us we're in the clear."

Dad tilted his head back toward Ryan. "We clear?"

"Yep." Ryan loved his dad's way of dealing with Ted, though he wished the man would put him in his place. As far as Ryan could tell, Ted did nothing to run the company. He was merely a strong back for the work.

Dad nodded sharply at Ryan's answer. "Let's go." He waved the file at Ted, trying to brush him out the door.

"That's it? No paper to sign, no proof of promise? No nothing? Just Ryan's word? Jesus, Dad. I'm tired of busting my ass for this business to let desk jockeys like him tell me what to do."

Apparently, David Kramer hit the breaking point. He snapped the edge of the folder under Ted's chin as if he were a child. "Enough of that bullshit. If I remember correctly, you, Earl, and your other brother sat around drinking during most of the job. When you and Earl fell into a pissing match over some damn football game a hundred years ago, he fired us. Fired us, because you couldn't let that lazy asshole be right. Then he gave us the bum's rush without letting me finish up the electrical, or at least cap off the wires. Nope. Both you and Earl wanted me and Brett out of there in a flash."

Ryan stood from his chair, moving closer to the two men. His father had never made a speech that long in his thirty-plus years. The red color climbing up Dad's neck didn't look like a healthy glow. Ryan prepped for action before things came to blows.

Ted's chest puffed up more and more as Dad went on. At this rate, they'd need a riot squad and two ambulances. Ryan sidestepped between them.

"Now, everyone take a breath." He glanced at Dad's bright red neck and Ted's inflated chest. "The Porter fire was not the fault of Kramer and Sons. I'm sure the insurance inspector will agree with my report. I already spoke with him after the fire."

His words fell on deaf ears. Dad crossed his arms, his eyes narrowed. "You know why we have a crappy rep in town? Not because of me. I'm a great carpenter and electrician, but as a contractor, you suck. Your brother ain't so bad, but you can't get your head out of your ass long enough to focus on the whole job. You're always distracted, trying to be in charge. Me and Brett are always cleaning up your mess. Hell, Ryan's better at it than you, and he ain't done half the training."

"Whatchu saying, Dad?" Ted almost sounded teary. "You saying I'm not good enough to work in your precious company? That I'm the whole problem why business is slow?"

Dad crossed his arms over his chest again. "Yep."

"You son of a..." Ted lunged at Dad and Ryan caught him before he did any damage. He grabbed his brother's fist, as he had with Earl a few days earlier. He twisted Ted's arm until he forced the man to face the door. Ryan pulled up on his brother's wrist, his other hand gripping the elbow.

"You remember this move, don't ya, Ted? I do. I wore a sling that whole summer." He kept his voice low and dangerous. Something Ted understood. "We will walk to the door with me holding your arm. You will leave the building, go home, and take a few days off of work. When you cool down, you can talk to Dad again, but only if I'm there. I won't allow you to hit Dad. And if I hear of you sneaking back over to Kramer and Sons before we talk, I'll get a restraining order."

They duck-walked to the door and Ryan released Ted's arm. Ted swung around, snorting through his nose like a bull. Ryan didn't flinch a millimeter. "You pencil necks..."

"Know about assault laws and have good lawyers," Ryan finished for him. "Go home. Think about it. You don't have to work for Dad. If construction isn't your thing..."

Ted huffed at him, turning back to go out the door. "What do you know?" He stomped away like a spoiled child. Maybe someone should have said it to his brother years ago.

He turned to his dad, ready to apologize for his brother again. Instead, he found his father next to him. The two watched Ted swagger down the hallway and out the front door. Dad sucked his teeth. "I'm gonna retire, son. Give you the business. You game?" Typical Dad, no fluff or buildup. Just the plain truth.

"Let me think about it, Dad."

"Fair enough."

Chapter Eleven

At a table in the parlor, Margaret adjusted the piles of paperwork before her. She wanted to be ready when Earl arrived. The lawyer's office might have been better. But the conversation with Earl needed to stay between the two of them. Having the meeting at the Inn ensured some safety for her, but the parlor only provided a hint of privacy.

And Earl, up in her room? No way.

She tapped her fitness tracker to check the time. Late, as always. The pay-per-view premium movie she rented for the kids (*PG-13, Mommy, without you? Yes!*) only lasted ninety minutes. Tardiness was the least of Earl's problems. She'd have to highlight a few bigger issues tonight, and she wasn't looking forward to it, not one bit.

The booming sound of the door slamming alerted her of his arrival. Who else would slam the door of a hundred-year-old inn? Sighing, she stood and moved to the doorway, hoping to cut him off before he roamed the halls.

"Margaret, where are ya?"

She waved from the doorframe, then crossed her arms over her chest.

He snorted, chest puffed out, hands on hips. "You enjoying spending my money on this place?" His sneer deepened.

She pressed her lips tight, not wanting to be drawn into an argument. "Follow me." Her teacher voice sounded in full form and not the nice kindergarten one. She spun on her heel and stalked back to the parlor.

"Whatever," he grumbled.

She glared over her shoulder, and he shut up. Again, she wondered what possessed her to marry him. She always fell for the sweet talk, the promises, and Earl was full of them. He'd delivered part of the promise, two kids, a nice house in a small town. Too bad he'd burned it down.

Her anger piquing, she slammed into her chair with a huff. Earl raised an eyebrow, sliding serenely into his chair. Another problem in their marriage, the angrier she was, the calmer, more flip he became. She was done with it. As the father of her children, he'd always be in her life, but he could be a distant presence.

"You're pissed," he said, the words without sarcasm or disdain. Margaret strained not to roll her eyes. "Didn't I take the kids that day? Ain't I been helping schlep them around while you putz around with that Kramer guy?" She sighed, opting not to strangle him.

"Yes, Earl, but we need to talk about the fire." She adjusted the paperwork in front of her. She hoped they'd agree to something verbally about the damages. More lawyers would prolong the problem, and she wanted her kids home for Christmas.

"You don't believe what your boyfriend said about me, do you? Those Kramers have always been fishy, scheming, tricky people. That's why I fired 'em."

Ah, an opening. "Let's talk about it," she said, grateful for her conflict resolution training at school. "What happened?" Maybe she should've recorded the conversation. But the deal she wanted to negotiate had to be quietly decided between her and Earl alone.

"That Ted. He told me I needed this kinda wire and that kinda insulation and these vents and stuff because of the fireplace unit. My buddy has the same one. Never had a problem. I told him he was full of shit, and he got big-chested and haughty with me. Asked me when I learned about construction. I told him the reason I hired him and his loser family was you'd never let me do it myself."

She smiled lightly, trying to hide an "I told you so" expression. "Why did you think that?"

Earl huffed, leaning back in his chair, arms crossed, ankles crossed. No hostility there. "You gotta always be by the book. Get a contractor, get a certified electrician, get references. You always gotta have your Is dotted and your Ts crossed. Ain't no one got time for that. We saved a bunch by me firing them. And you didn't know nothing..." He halted, hedging.

"Yeah, *you* fired them. You said it in front of Ryan Kramer, and there's no taking it back. Let's talk about it. He has proof the Kramers left the job early. Did you hire someone else? Do you have any proof of who finished the job?"

His brow furrowed. "Told ya. I did it. I closed up the wall and hooked up the stuff, the lights, TV, cable, and the fireplace. No biggie."

He didn't understand. "The electrical wasn't complete, Earl."

"Looked done to me." He shrugged. "They shoulda finished it."

She leaned toward him. "You fired them." She spoke calmly, though her jaw clamped down on the last word. He sputtered, and her patience hit the wall. She held up a hand, and he actually stopped. "Let's focus on the situation we're in now."

Earl, the nervy asshole, laughed. "What? You gonna sue me?"

"I realize you no longer own the house, but there's the real possibility the insurance won't cover anything." The words seemed to have no effect on him as she expected.

"And?" He rolled his wrist in a circle.

"And we have to pay for it. Out of pocket. It's Christmas." She hissed out the last word. Sometimes, she had to spell it.

"No, I don't. You gotta pay for it. It's your house now." He smirked, thinking he'd one-upped her.

Margaret grimaced. "But you're responsible for the fire. Your children live in that house. You should help me fund the repairs."

"Guess we'll need to renegotiate custody again. Did you file the paperwork, or did it burn up in the fire?" He winked.

Narrowing her gaze, she blasted him with the full brunt of her wrath. She was sick of the games, tired of playing with him, the Kramers, Ryan—everyone. Selling the house as-is and moving the kids to a new town, like Ballston or Ilion, sounded like a good solution to this mess. "I went back into the fire specifically to find it."

"You what?" A tremor of fear polluted his words. "You went back in for the custody stuff?"

"I worked hard to get the terms I wanted." She slapped the papers next to her. "You wanna renegotiate with me?"

He stared at the charred papers and swallowed hard. Finally, the man understood how Momma Bear she could be.

"I want full custody of the kids. You can have visitation once a month. No more. And it has to be here in Stonewater."

"You think you can negotiate that shit now? We spent weeks at the lawyers in paperwork hell. You think..."

She cut him off, standing. "I think your negligence caused a fire in the home where your children live. I have proof and witnesses to your confession. I'll go to my lawyer and redo the forms with the new information."

"Huh, blackmail from you. That surprises me." He narrowed his gaze, his fingers twitching.

"Not blackmail. Reality. Take responsibility, one way or another." She paused. "I think we're done here." She made a pretense of organizing the paperwork. The pile represented more than the custody paperwork. It included estimates for the damage, a rough one from a guy at the box lumber store. The man gave her a list of materials—the price astronomical.

"Where the hell do you think I'm going to find the money?" Earl twitched all over now. Money had always been a sticky issue in their marriage.

"I don't care. It's not blackmail, Earl. The fact is, the insurance company won't come through if you were negligent. The Kramers aren't responsible. So, you'll have to pay. And if you don't, I can go to the lawyers and have them taken away.

Who's going to allow a man who caused a fire in his children's home to have custody?"

She paused, watching him fidget. He hated being wrong, hated when she knew more and argued better. But as she was no longer his wife, she didn't care about hurting his ego. Giving him a minute to absorb her words, she went on.

"The claim doesn't have to go in," she said. "I can forget to submit it."

He stood from his chair and began a furious pace around the room. "You're winning either way. I don't help, you get the kids. I do help, you get the kids. You got me pinned and you love it."

"Earl," she said quietly, her gaze down on the papers in front of her. "Be honest. Custody of Jill and Mikey... is it something you really want? Do you want to drive here every weekend to collect them? Do you want to shuffle them to school from Albany every Monday morning? It'd be tough to make it work on a good day. Weekend custody without you living in town is difficult at best.

"Take the once-a-month option, and I'll let you off the hook for the fire." She folded her hands on the table. Earl always required think-time. As a kindergarten teacher, she knew full well the value of allowing someone to work out a problem on their own.

"Yer saying if I do the one weekend, I don't gotta pay for the damage? Horseshit. You'll come after me some other way and empty my bank account like you always do." He huffed, turning away.

Using her gentlest new-student voice, she said, "Earl, you know I've never asked you for much in the way of money. And when I do, it's for the kids. Please, let me have this, and you won't be responsible for thousands of dollars in damage. Not to mention the gossip from the whole town about your role in the fire. Let me mop it up, and you can walk away."

He sat down again, hard, his chin in his hand. "I didn't mean to do it," he whined, as if he wanted to say sorry but couldn't bring himself to utter the words.

If Margaret had a dollar for every time that tone spilled from his lips, she'd be rich.

"I know," she conceded, pushing the custody paperwork toward him. "Sign and initial where I indicated, and the lawyer will take care of the rest."

He turned to her, his face drawn. He loved their kids but had a hard time expressing it. Grabbing the pen, he flipped pages of the document. "And you won't ask for money for the fire?" He held the pen poised to sign.

"Nope, I'll take care of it."

The pen hit the table. "How?"

Sighing, Margaret dug in. "I can do after-school classes, teach summer school, do some babysitting in the neighborhood. I'll handle it."

Earl took up the pen again, rolling his eyes all the while. "Fine. I'll sign it, but I ain't sending any extra money down the road." He scrawled his signature on the document.

Margaret snatched it from him before he changed his mind. "I'd settle for the child support you owe me." She smiled at him, a nasty one, and didn't care she was being a bitch. "I think we're done." The finality in her last word reverberated through the room.

"Typical Margaret. Sweet one second, a total cunt the next."

She had no more patience. "Yeah, yeah..."

"I want something in return." Earl screwed his face up, either thinking or trying to look mean. Margaret was done.

"What? Getting out of thousands of dollars in repairs isn't enough?"

He huffed. "I want those tools I left in the garage. And the lawnmower, and the snowblower, and..."

She held up a hand to cut him off. "Hold up there. You can't just raid my garage. Let's go over to the house and you can choose a few things to take. A few." He pouted but agreed.

They took separate cars, leaving the kids upstairs, watching their movie. Margaret figured a quick trip back home, clean out the junk in the garage, and get rid of Earl at the same time.

At the house, the driveway had way too many tire tracks for an unoccupied house. Margaret dismissed it as the fading light filled the sky. It looked abandoned in the snow, with its plastic sheeting and scorch marks.

As she and Earl rounded on the garage, she heard voices outside on the lawn. Male voices and Margaret froze. There was a hole in her house, after all. Anyone could remove the plastic and walk right in. Earl must have sensed her nervousness.

"Don't you worry, baby. I'll take care of it." *Cunt one second, baby the next.* Earl's logic always twisted her in knots. He tiptoed from the garage around the side of the house with something like stealth. He held a finger to his lips, then cupped his ear. She shook her head at the over-the-top machismo of the act.

She grabbed Mikey's wooden bat from the sports rack and followed Earl to the doorway. As usual, she'd handle the problem.

Chapter Twelve

Ryan glanced at his brother. Not the best way to mend fences, but they always connected better when talking shop. "What do you think?"

Ted scratched his head. "You sure we ain't paying for this?" Ryan nodded. "Then I think about a week, depending on scheduling. She's already got the contract set up with Dad?"

"Yeah, about that..." Ryan scrubbed the back of his neck. Would Margaret even take his call, much less sign a contract? He glanced at his brother. Behind him, a huge shape loomed in the twilight. Instinctively, Ryan grabbed his brother's shirt and pulled him backward, the two of them stumbling back a half-dozen steps.

The figure's arms flailed, backlit by the house lights. Definitely a male, but... "What the hell do you think..." The words were cut off by the sound of a wooden bat thwacking something solid. "Hey!" the man squealed, jumping back.

Ryan snapped his light over to highlight Earl Porter cowering next to his ex-wife. A smile spread across Ryan's lips.

"Jesus, Earl. It's the Kramers," she said. Ryan's flashlight caught her disgusted look and the bat in her hand. Was it for him or Earl?

"Ya didn't have to hit me, though," Earl complained, and Ryan stifled a laugh.

"Please. Don't be a baby." Margaret raised the bat to point at Ryan and Ted. "And what are you two doing on my property after dark?" Her tone was all business. Ryan loved it. Of the four of them, she was the toughest person here.

"I wanted to show Ted the damage and discuss how long the repairs might take. And as for dark, considering the sun goes down at 4:10..." He shrugged. "Besides, I didn't think you'd be here." His last words held some serious mortification. But showing a little remorse for trespassing might help. "I apologize, ma'am."

Margaret snorted, but Earl cut her off before she said any more. "You two shitters get the hell off my property. No one hired you. No one asked you here. Now git."

"Not your house, Earl"—Margaret's only comment.

"I mean it now," Earl continued as if she hadn't spoken. He grabbed the kid bat right out of her hand. She cursed in protest, but he didn't give it back. Instead, he brandished it at Ryan and Ted. "Git!"

Ryan slapped his forehead. *What the hell?* Earl acted as if he were still back in high school.

Not to be outdone, Ted stepped up. "What's your problem, Earl? We came here to help. To see about the damage you caused. You made the mess, and we're trying to fix it." Ted huffed, his chest inflating again.

Earl edged forward until the two stood inches apart. "What are you saying, Ted? You think it's my mess? I'm pretty sure your dad screwed up the wiring. In fact, I know he did. I had to fix it before *I*"—He thumped his chest—"finished the job. And now you think I'm gonna let you two touch my house? Think again."

Margaret repeated, "Not your house."

Ted stepped forward. Now the two stood toe to toe. The smell of testosterone poisoned the air. The men snarled at each other, throwing curses and insults, accomplishing nothing. When Earl twitched the bat, Ryan knew it was time to step in.

Deftly, he snagged it from Earl's grasp and stepped back. "I think that's enough, boys. Stand down." With quiet words, he tried to mimic his dad's authoritative voice, and surprisingly, his brother relented.

But Earl kept talking. "You were nothing back in high school, and you're still nothing now. Trying to big a big shot. But you're a loser. That's why Cheryl left you. You're the worst contractor in town and everyone knows it. And I'm gonna tell 'em how you burned my house down." He sneered like a little kid.

Something inside Ryan snapped. Righteous fury exploded inside him. How dare this punk trash-talk his family. He ought to slap the stupid expression off Earl's face.

Instead, he put a palm on his brother's chest. "Let me, Ted." He turned to Earl. "My brother had nothing to do with the fire, Earl. And you know it. He did a bang-up job on the carpentry for this project and dozens of others across town. You won't find a better guy around to fix your carpentry problems. But you wanna be a dick about it? Fine. We're leaving. With that attitude, don't expect Ted to ever come back. Your loss."

Ryan tugged at his brother's sleeve as he turned to leave. Not how he planned for tonight to go. He'd hoped to talk with

Margaret, find an understanding with her. But Earl... what an ass. Something about him fired up the fraternal love.

"You've got a lotta nerve, you little shit. No one talks to me that way," Earl snarled. Ryan barely glanced at the man as he passed the bat back to Margaret. Out of the corner of his eye, he saw Earl twist. Instincts kicked in and Ryan spun. He clocked Earl in the jaw as hard as he could. He only registered Earl's upraised fist after his own fist connected.

Earl hit the ground with a thump, spread eagle on his back. The three stood over his prone body. Even after a minute, the man still hadn't moved.

"I think he's out, little bro," Ted said with a snicker. "You want us to remove this trash from your lawn, Ms. Porter?"

Margaret smirked. "Nah. Leave him there. But you both should be going." Her chin tilted up and her arms folded, the bat firmly in her grip.

Ryan would have to find another way to win Margaret back. For now, he'd take the points he scored for his family. He and Ted walked back to the truck, settled in, and drove from the property. They remained silent for several minutes, Ryan deep in his head about what to do next for Margaret, her house, and her kids' ruined Christmas.

Ted spoke up, "You didn't have to defend me there, bro."

Ryan spoke without thinking. "Yeah, I did. That ass wanted to trash-talk you all over town. You're a good carpenter, bro. Everyone knows it."

"Yeah, but we've gotten some bad press and now that house..." He sighed, sounding defeated.

"I said you were a good carpenter, Ted, not a good project manager. Maybe we could use some fresh blood at Kramer."

"You?"

"Me." Ryan waited for his brother's response.

"It might work," he said quietly, no derision in his voice.

Huh.

After so many years, all he needed to do to fix family relations was to coldcock some asshole and then compliment his brother. *Who'd-a thunk?*

Chapter Thirteen

Margaret sat at the little desk in her room at the Greenview Inn. A dozen documents laid out before her, including her weekly checklist. Most items had a line through them, but a few sported huge red circles. File paperwork with lawyer—check. File adjusted paperwork with insurance—check.

But the to-do list remained long. Re-purchase Christmas presents, get a new tree, find a repairman for the house, call parents for a loan?

She stared hard at the last one. Staying at the Inn was a godsend, and everyone there had been overly accommodating because of the fire. But the cost during the busy holiday season exceeded her budget. And the insurance wouldn't reimburse her. The money represented either presents for the kids, or a portion of the repair.

Earl'd never help. His backlogged child support payments showed his lack of responsibility. So much for cable, Wi-Fi, not to mention Friday night pizza.

Margaret sighed, her shoulders slumping as she put her head on the desk. Even if she were to max out the one credit card she owned, she didn't have enough to pay for the repairs to the house. With Christmas and the Inn bill, she was sunk.

The room door slammed, knocking Margaret out of her pity party. Mikey dashed inside and threw himself on her lap. "We're going home now, right?" His wide grin warmed her heart. Margaret couldn't blame him. Breakfast here at the Inn was enough to make the worst Scrooge smile. Of course, Mikey hadn't seen the inside of the house since the fire.

She'd tried to clean up some after the ridiculous confrontation between the Kramers and Earl. Such macho posturing, though she enjoyed how Ryan flattened Earl with one blow. Never mind that she hated him for screwing up her financial situation.

His actions held some logic. Saving the family business, oh, and that whole telling the truth thing. She wished he'd talked to her first before confronting Earl. Perhaps they could have... oh, she didn't know, found a better solution, tricked Earl into paying?

Something.

Used to be, sleeping with someone earned you favors.

Margaret snorted at the idea. Not her style at all. She never asked for favoritism or special treatment for anything, especially sexual favors, even in her marriage. But for once, she hoped some man would do good by her in a time of trouble. Earl left her high and dry, but when Ryan screwed her, it cut her to the bone.

Squeezing her son, she kissed his forehead. "Yes, home again."

"Jiggity, jig!" Mikey screamed and dashed around the room, collecting random toys and socks.

Margaret watched, an amused smile on her lips. She caught Jill's gaze. The teen stood in the doorway, shaking her head at her brother. "Anyway..." Jill rolled her eyes. Typical fourteen. "I spoke with Emil..."

"You mean Mr. Russo?" Jill's crush on the innkeeper deepened with each day they stayed.

"Yeah, whatever. He gave me the recipe for the apple pie. I want to try it when we're home, okay?" She glared at her mother as if Margaret might deny her daughter the right to use a recipe a handsome man taught her.

Margaret repressed a grin. "I guess. We'll need to hit the grocery store," she said as she scooped up the papers and tossed them into her purse. *One less thing to pack.*

"Duh, Mom." Jill threw herself down on the bed, phone in hand. "After four days, you think any of the food will be good?" She made an exaggerated gagging gesture before turning her back.

Fourteen—so fun.

"You quit already?" David Kramer leaned back in his desk chair, his ankles crossed. He twitched a toothpick from one side of his mouth to the other.

"Not exactly, Dad. I spoke with the mayor about my position and your retirement. I'm part-time anyway. She knew I'd need a full-time job at some point." Ryan didn't want to step out on the job he'd just begun, but if Dad was serious about retirement, then there was no time like the present.

"I don't want ya getting a bad rep about town. How's about I wait until Mayor Anthony finds a replacement? Some guy without as many conflicts of interest." Dad's wry grin warmed Ryan.

He shook his head. "If you insist, Dad. But in the meantime, can I borrow some supplies?"

Dad leaned further back in his chair. "Borrow, no. Buy, yes." He grinned, and Ryan threw his hat at him.

Chapter Fourteen

Margaret pulled into the driveway, her temper already flaring. Another truck parked at her house. She was tired of these surprise visits from every guy in town. Who now? Another Kramer? Her old high school boyfriend? Grumbling, she slammed the car door shut.

"Kids, grab the groceries while I deal with this," she called over her shoulder as she stalked around the house.

"Sure, Ma. Just dump me with him and $200 worth of food. I'm not responsible if he eats the brownies." Jill stood with her hands on her hips, tapping her foot. Margaret waved her off. Strange trucks took precedence over pissy teens and brownie-stealing kiddos.

"Hey!" Margaret snapped as she rounded the corner of the house. "What do you think..." The words died in her throat. Plywood, sawhorses, and two by fours covered the ground. The plastic that had screened the hole in the wall lay on the snow, and someone was sawing away at the damaged wood.

The truck in the driveway wasn't Earl's van, but if he borrowed... "Hey," she called again. "What do you think you're doing?" An idiot working out here in the cold and snow without permission. It must be...

Ryan.

Margaret stopped dead. Words died in her throat at the sight of him in a winter coat, gloves, and wool hat under a construction helmet. "Wha..." was the only sound to escape her.

"Damn," he said, rubbing the back of his neck. "I thought you wouldn't be home for another hour or more. I asked Emil to stall you."

"Is that why he tried to feed us?" Margaret huffed. "I told him off, thinking he wanted to weasel another meal out of my thin wallet. I'm such an ass."

Ryan tossed down his hand saw and crossed to her, one arm wrapping around her shoulder. "Nah, you forget some of us are good guys. Like Emil."

Margaret pursed her lips. "Like you."

Ryan shrugged. "If the shoe fits.

"Nice guys who break into my house and help my ex-husband get out of paying for repairs?" She tapped her foot, á la Jill. But there was no bite in her words. She knew Ryan had done the right thing. Well, except he'd included Earl in the discussion.

Ryan squared her in front of him, one hand on each shoulder. "Yes, nice guys who realized they screwed up about your insurance claim. Nice guys who won't lie about things like this and who care about you. Nice guys who want you and your kids to have a Christmas without a hole in your house. Nice guys who wanna fix it."

A warmth spread over her chest, but Margaret couldn't give in to him. Not yet. "Nice guys who think they can fix everything usually make it worse." Earl had seemed like a nice guy, merely misunderstood, and she paid for that mistake for years. She wasn't walking down the same road again.

"Yes, ma'am," Ryan said quietly. He released her, and she resisted the urge to curl closer to him in the cold. To feel his warm arms around her, to hear him say everything will work out, that he wasn't blowing smoke. "If you'll let me, Ms. Porter..."

"It's Ms. Porter now?" She cocked an eyebrow, but he held up a finger, making her wait.

"If you'll allow me to present a gift to you and your family." He waved a hand at the open wall, tucking the other behind him.

"A busted wall? Thanks. I've got one." She took a step, pretending to leave. Ryan had something up his sleeve. She wanted nothing more than to throw him down in the snow and thank him for even being there, but she waited, letting him play his hand.

"Ah, but Daisy..." He flipped his hand out from behind his back and with a snap, a bouquet of white daisies appeared, something out of a magician's hat.

Flowers? Daisies. Man, this guy was good. She played stoic, though. "What?" she asked as he pushed the flowers into her hands. He grasped her arm and pulled her forward, showing her the view through the hole.

Inside her living room, her children sat before a six-foot, fully decorated Christmas tree surrounded by presents. The exact vision she'd had earlier of Ryan with her family.

Margaret's mouth dropped open. "How?" she gasped.

"There's a big hole in your wall, and the tree fit right in." He held out a hand for her and they stepped through the gap.

The space remained a mess, with a soggy carpet and charred walls. But the tree lit up the room like... well, like Christmas. "Those are battery-powered LED lights. Safe and easy to use. No wires."

"No wires." She breathed. Her chest constricted and tears burned in her eyes. "Ryan..." She didn't know what to think. He saved Christmas. "You'll repair the wall?" The words poured out of her before she realized what she was asking. She put a hand over her mouth, embarrassed.

"Yes. Might take a bit with my other two jobs, but every spare minute I have, I'll be here, helping, in any way I can." He ran a finger down her cheek, saying a thousand things with the tiny gesture.

Her heart filled with emotion as Mikey discovered a huge firetruck under the tree and squealed with delight. "I can't ask," she said.

"You're not," Ryan whispered in her ear. "I'm giving." His warm breath on her ear sent fire through her veins. Should she let him repair her house? And make such a grand gesture after they'd only known each other...

"It's Christmas," he said. She glanced at the tree, the presents—not tons, but a few, and the soft twinkling from the colored lights. The room, though messy, finally had the holiday spirit, thanks to Ryan. He pointed upward. A sprig of mistletoe hung over the gap in the wall.

She smiled, her heart overflowing with the possibilities of the future. And the perfect placement of the sprig. "Christmas." She swallowed the lump of emotion in her throat. "It's the little things." Touching her forehead to his, she said, "Thank you, Ryan. I..."

"Eww. Don't look, squirt," Jill interrupted.

Margaret turned to blast the girl, but as Ryan caught her chin, he placed his finger to her lips. "Merry Christmas." And he kissed her until her toes curled.

The End

Check out these titles by Ginny Frost

The Oakwood Tavern Series

The Bar Scene, Oakwood Tavern 1

Terese Brock manages the Oakwood Tavern with style and grace. Unfortunately, she's trying to avoid her employer's IRS disaster and her own debts. She needs a new job—fast. Terese hopes to land an executive position at the new conference center, the perfect solution to all her money woes.

For months, Drew Drake has admired Terese from afar, but she doesn't know he exists. He's thrilled when his humor and persistence catch her eye. And when she takes him home, he discovers she's everything he expected, and so much more.

Drew fails to mention he's the heir to one of the most successful businesses in town, the force behind the new conference center. Rather than clue her in, he decides to let her get to know the real him. When she walks into her interview, ready to kick ass and take names, her universe shatters.

Behind the desk sits her boy-toy, Drew.

Swindled, Oakwood Tavern 2

For years, Marley Volkov's survival depended on conning people out of their life savings. One look into Alan Reid's pained eyes, with his soiled reputation and heap of financial problems, awakens a new empathy inside her. She renounces grifting forever and not just because every inch of her burns to be with him. But his association with her and her checkered past will drag him further into the gutter. To save herself, to save him, she must walk away. Walk away from the unbridled desire he inspires, from the passion and sympathy that feel like home.

Alan Reid is buried to the neck in money issues. The understanding and compassion he finds in Marley is the exact thing he needs at the completely wrong time. Everything about her makes his blood run hot. She's smart, irresistible, and a criminal. Why is the only person who's ever shown him sympathy have to be a con artist? He can't be with her, but he's compelled to save her from herself.

Stranded, Oakwood Tavern 3

Where the hell is Conrad?

While his business partners back at The Oakwood Tavern think he's on the run for tax evasion, for Conrad Bennett, it's a whole other story. One that includes being stranded on an island in the South Pacific with no cell phone, no money, and no passport.

Good thing he just slept with the only woman on the island with a plane.

Vivian Costa has her own problems. She's on this remote island for a much needed, much overdue, self-imposed exile. But now her one-night stand wants not only a ride off the island, but to find out who has set him up. So much for laying low and hiding out. Vivian knows she should walk away, but there's something about Conrad that won't let her.

It's time to figure out how to rescue each other.

When Hearts Collide, Oakwood Tavern 4, Sandy Bay 5

Planning and organizing the wedding this weekend left Stacey Montgomery little time for fun. She's woefully behind on her Bucket List from the bridal shower. Right now, on the plane to Massachusetts, it's her last chance to cross off number three. Luckily, there's a hottie sitting next to her, and he looks promising. And if her plan succeeds, she might invite him for all the other winter activities on the list.

After working through a criminal IRS audit at his job in Iverton, Eric Holmes could use some rest and relaxation. Usually, bad luck plows him flat like a steamroller, but this time his friend Pete caught the bad juju. With his bestie in a cast from a skiing accident, Eric gladly took Pete's place to tend bar at a destination wedding on the Atlantic coast. Then, he sat next to the most beautiful woman—blonde, curvy, and...

She just asked him to join the mile-high club

Gulp.

But how can he say no?

Stonewater Stories

The Carriage House, Stonewater Stories Book 0.5

Homeless, jobless, and newly single, Cheryl Winston-Bristol finds herself back at her oppressive childhood home. Even at the Carriage House of their estate, she can't escape her overbearing mother and tyrant of a grandfather from making her life miserable. That is until she discovers her high school crush, Ted Kramer, repairing the steps. The dozen years of handyman repairs have molded him into quite a hunk.

Ted working around her house every day? Yes, thank you.

Desperate for the work, Ted Kramer of Kramer and Sons agreed to take the job at the Winston-Bristol's Carriage House. Ted is both excited and terrified since most of their family hates his. Then he discovers Cheryl is home and living in the Carriage House. Working in the same place with the beautiful, classy Cheryl terrifies and excites him. He can handle seeing the charming Cheryl all summer, can't he?

In this prequel to the Stonewater Stories, learn how Ted and Cheryl found each other. To hear their happily ever after, read all of the Stonewater Stories.

Christmas Affair, Stonewater Stories Book 2

Josephine Lockwood spent her entire life in a sickbed being coddled by her anxious mother. Finally, after receiving the correct diagnosis for her illness, she's standing on the edge of a new adventure. She's finished her audition program for an online gaming platform and is poised to move out of her family home. But she must attend her mother's annual Christmas party.

Brett Kramer, a hard-working handyman, is finishing up renovations at the Excelsior Hotel in Iverton when Jo drops into his life. She's cute, friendly, and totally intriguing. Too bad he's at work. The family contracting business is suffering thanks to a bogus complaint, and he doesn't want any whiff of impropriety to taint the current contract.

But when Jo flees from her mother's party, Brett steps in to help her escape, disregarding his business's reputation.

Their departure only complicates the situation. A snowstorm, sibling rivalry, and an overprotective mother forces them together and tears them apart. Jo and Brett must find a balance to make their relationship more than a Christmas Affair.

Christmas Baby, Stonewater Stories Book 3

He'd heard the rumors she was back in town. He had to see for himself.

As Ted Kramer steeled himself to knock on the hotel room door, the last thing he was prepared to see was the woman who shattered him holding a baby. Cheryl Winston-Bristol had been the love of his life. And when she abruptly left town last year after their secret summer romance, it destroyed him. He couldn't eat. Couldn't sleep. Couldn't work. Yet here she is, baby and all. His baby. Merry Christmas to him.

When Cheryl realized she was pregnant, she knew her controlling and manipulative grandfather would never accept a Kramer child into his family. The feud between the Kramers and Winston-Bristols had dragged on for forty years and as long as that cantankerous man was alive, it would continue raging. Except now he's dead, and Cheryl has taken the opportunity to return to Stonewater for the services. She knows she needs to tell her mother—and Ted—about the baby, but she never wanted him to find out about his daughter like this, though.

Maybe, just maybe, baby Harper will be the Christmas gift these families need to move on and find love again.

New Year's Miracle, Stonewater Stories Book 4

This past Christmas, Beverly Winston-Bristol's entire world has flipped on its side. Her beloved father passed away, and her errant daughter, Cheryl, has returned with a new baby, a Baby Kramer at that.

Beverly must heal old wounds for the sake of Baby Harper. If she continues her vendetta against David Kramer and his sons, she'll not only lose Cheryl again but her first grandchild as well. But being near David still hurts. Now that they are grandparents together, can Bev deal with having him back in her life?

On New Year's Eve, Harper's crib collapses. Alone with the baby, Beverly has no choice but to call David to rescue her.

Enjoy this sweet edition to the Stonewater Stories.

The Mortar & Pestle Series

Artist: A Second Chance Romance

Lexi Pintari is stuck in a dead-end cubicle job that is slowly killing her. She tucked away her passion for art when the love of her life ghosted her after college. Witnessing her lack of motivation, Lexi's best friend drags her to an art retreat for much-needed reflection and inspiration. Though knowing her ex-boyfriend is an artist-in-residence there, Lexi agrees to go.

Unfortunately, her metal-goth style and enthusiasm for graphic comics clash with the pastel-scarf-wearing, tea-sipping participants, making her ex the least of her problems.

Cole MacDougall is blocked. His rise to the top of the modern art scene is crushed by a missing muse. He is desperate to paint again, but the canvas remains blank. Due to the shortage of patronage revenue, he is forced to put up with the groupie-students. Until he sees a woman standing out like a sore thumb in ripped jeans and a leather jacket. Lexi. Hope blooms that he can renew his passion through her.

About the Author

Ginny Frost is an indie author with three great series. She writes contemporary romance with a sexy, funny kick. In her downtime, she plays clerk at the local library—the perfect job to feed her reading addiction.

She lives in upstate NY with her very own kindhearted ogre, their two brilliant and creative children, and an evil cat named Flash.

You can find her on various social media sites and her website: www.ginnyfrost.com